Landscapes Of A New Land

Landscapes Of A New Land

Fiction By Latin American Women

Edited by Marjorie Agosin

White Pine Press

ISBN 0–934834–96–2 (Paper)

Publication of this book was made possible, in part, by grants from the New York State Council on the Arts and the National Endowment for the Arts.

Design by Watershed Design
Cover artwork by Emma Alvarez Pineiro

Printed in the United States of America.

ACKNOWLEDGEMENTS

The editor thanks all the writers and translators that so willingly collaborated in this anthology. Their generosity as well as their spirits can be found in these landscapes of new words.

"Plaza Maua"—from Clarice Lispector; *Soulstorm*. Copyright 1974 by Clarice Lispector, 1989 by Alexis Levitin. Translated by Alexis Levitin.

"Genealogies"—from Margo Glanz: *Genealogies*, forthcoming from Serpent's Tail (London).

WHITE PINE PRESS
P.O. Box 236
Buffalo, N.Y. 14201

76 Center Street
Fredonia, N.Y. 14063

This book is dedicated to my grandmother, Josefina,
a fantastic letter writer and teller of tales.

Landscapes Of A New Land

Contents

Landscapes Of A New Land

Introduction

Throughout history, women have always been close to language. Transmitters of legends, healers, magicians and fortune tellers, women possess a tapestry of stories that are slowly beginning to be transcribed. Curiously, with the advent of authoritarian governments in Latin America, women have left the private spaces of house, church, and marketplace to begin to poeticize their experiences through the written word that had previously been denied to them. We must not forget that even with the Cuban Revolution and the political effervescence that followed in the 1960s, the arts in Latin America continued to be dominated by men. Women were only allowed to participate through their relationships with men: the "companero," the boss, and the patriarch.

In the 1970s, Latin America awoke to the voices of legendary women writers such as Maria Luisa Bombal. Her writings were reprinted, and North American universities held conferences on her work. Her books and stories were translated into different languages. Along with the rediscovery of our literary grandmothers came the emergence of the voices of a new generation of women. Luisa Valenzuela, the most translated writer in this collection, began to publish stories, novels, and tales of insanity, such as the collection *Aquí pasan cosas raras* (*Strange Things Happen Here*), as well as epigrams, conversations, and collages concerning the Argentine political situation under the military junta in the Seventies.

Carmen Naranjo, from Costa Rica, began to publish her allegories of power and its banality, using subtle tones and language. Voices were also born that linked the intense lyricism of expression with the inertia of the middle class that forces women into conformity, submission, or evasion through dreams and imagination. In her story "I Love My Husband" Nelida Piñon from Brazil expresses the gloomy condition of women: "They salute me too for nourishing a man who dreams of mansions, shanties, and huts and so makes the nation progress. And that is why I am the shadow of the man whom everyone says I love."

The idea for this collection arose from the pressing need to rescue the voices of the great women of letters that are scarcely known in English, such as the Chilean Marta Brunet, Yolanda Bedregal from Bolivia, and others, distinguished authors in their own countries but little recognized abroad. This collection also attempts to show the wide range of themes, images, and uses of language encountered in the new territories of the Latin American narrative written by women.

The stories are not arranged chronologically or geographically, but instead by the images and voices that reflect the eclectic nature and energy of these women. The collection begins with Maria Luisa Bombal, who was widely recognized in Latin America and in the United States during the 1940s. The prose poem "Sky, Sea and Earth" alludes to the magical secrets and prophesies that are linked to the mythical image of women. Nevertheless, here, the woman writer assumes the identity of expert as well as possessor of the earth and of words: "I know about many things of which no one knows. I am familiar with an infinite number of tiny and magical secrets from the sea and from the earth."

The collection continues with fragments from the work of Margo

Glantz, a Mexican author, journalist, professor of literature, and cultural attache in London. This wanderer also elaborates and recounts her life through the written word. *The Genealogies*, of which a sixth edition has already been published in her country, alludes to the porous, rebellious, and eclectic quality of so many writers: "And I have written my book because my parents' life was not enclosed in precise outlines and suddenly my own life had nothing to hold on to. So I went back to my memories and after to my parents' memories in order to be able to reshape certain aspects of the country in which I was born, this country Mexico so far away from my parents' country, Russia."

The second part of this anthology groups together stories linked by the theme of love and its mysteries. The section begins with the mysterious prose of Yolanda Bedregal in "Good Evening, Agatha," where the ambiguous tone and surreal character of the narrative emphasize the connection of these women with magic and the incredible. The man, dreamed or real in the story, is a leit motif in these texts that attempts to instill a meaningful order on complicated human relationships.

"Destination" by the Brazilian author Patricia Bins, like the work of Bedregal, expresses the author's experiences through the poetics of ambiguity and suggestive visual images. "Destination" is a prose poem that attempts through words to alter, reconstruct, and improve a life shared in a noble, sincere manner. Her contemporary, Hilda Hilst, also constructs a language of complex metaphors to express alienation and solitude.

It is this same obstacle of meaning and of fulfillment that is profiled in the pages of Nelida Pinon's "I Love My Husband" and in "The Key," written by another Brazilian, Lygia Fagundes Telles. "The Key" is a subtly ironic story in which social relations are sketched in a world where the predominant values lie in the power of appearances. "The Message" by the Mexican Elena Poniatowska evokes the nostalgia of young love with a language filled with reminiscences of an era gone by. In "Solitude of Blood" by Marta Brunet, the couple is formed through a different social medium than in the other stories, Nevertheless, conjugal happiness is nonexistent and violence invades the woman's personal space. Lispector, undoubtedly Brazil's most distinguished woman writer, incorporates in "Plaza Maua" a tender lyricism together with a poignant reality that enwraps her female characters.

The third part of the anthology brings to light themes relevant to Latin American culture, stories that have to do with political, social, authoritarian, and repressive power. "The Open Letter" by Helena Araujo from Colombia opens this section. This piece clearly profiles the corruption of Latin American governments that torture and violate the laws that are most essential to their citizens. Alicia Steimberg's "Cecilia's Last Will and Testament" reveals with a haunting clarity the unknown fate of the disappeared, the thousands of people who continue to occupy physical and emotional spaces in the literary, as well as the political, imagination of its readers.

Carmen Naranjo's story, "The Compulsive Couple of the House on the Hill," refers to the politics of the people and enunciates a profound social criticism of an entire society dominated by the false ideologies of social charity. Naranjo's piece serves as a complement to Araujo's story and to that of Luisa Valenzuela, "The Snow White Guard," which illustrates the absurd, alien, and cruel life of a police officer. Alonso, an enigmatic figure in the Cuban cultural scene, continues to transform reality, as we can observe in "Cage Number One."

Children's literature also plays a central role in this anthology, for women have always been oral transmitters of literature when reading stories to their children.

"Jimena's Fair," written by the Peruvian Laura Riesco, alludes to this fragmentary world divided behind the symbolic bars of exploitation. The bars also symbolize a divided country, where the rich inhabitants are trapped as well as the poor, enclosed and fearful of their own riches as well as of their roles as exploiters. Another kind of exploitation can be observed in Jacqueline Balcell's "The Enchanted Raisin," where the highly regarded values of matrimonial love are transformed into an almost feminist rage.

With her unforgettable descriptions of the desert of Atacama,

Amalia Rendic creates an appropriate atmosphere for her tale, "A Child, A Dog, The Night." She shows that, despite class conflicts, it is still possible to find human kindness through the souls of children.

The collection ends with the characteristic elements of much of Latin American literature—elements that fluctuate between irrationality, insanity, and the magical-diabolical. Silvina Ocampo, distinguished Argentine writer and precursor to the fantastical literature in her country along with Adolfo Bioy Casares and Jorge Luis Borges, appears with the extraordinary story "The Servant's Slave," where magic takes on an evil aura, and human nature with its envies and intrigues is faithfully portrayed.

Along with Ocampo, another Argentine belonging to a younger generation, Elvira Orphée, also plays with the universe of magic and the absurd. The story that appears in this collection, "The Beguiling Ladies," reflects this unreal dimension. For example, Dona Eulogia's apparently beautiful house possesses certain frightening and ambiguous resonances.

Cristina Peri Rossi, in "The Museum of Futile Endeavors," also discusses absurdity by objectifying and incorporating banal experiences, such as the man who wanted to fly or the man who desperately tried to get a woman to love him until he finally killed himself.

What does Peri Rossi suggest with this phantasmagoric museum of wasted efforts? Our inability to preserve history or the fact that history becomes, lives, invents itself and can never by pigeon-holed in enormous, dusty, forgotten annals.

These narrators show that written history contains the lyricism of poetry and the rational insanity of passion. They teach us that History and these smaller histories spring from an intimate, delicate conscience where memory attempts not only to preserve the great events of History such as wars, conquests, and triumphs, but also in the daily history that is created in a park, in the depths of the ocean, or in the ancient icon of the family.

The landscapes profiled in this collection reveal an original world where nothing is useless, where everything can be a way of introduc-

ing new spaces, where women can inscribe themselves in a living museum and in the landscapes of a brave new world for all of us.
—Marjorie Agosin

Translated by Janice Molloy

Genealogies

Sky, Sea And Earth

Maria Luisa Bombal

I know about many things of which no one knows. I am familiar with an infinite number of tiny and magical secrets from the sea and from the earth.

I know, for example, that in the ocean depths, much lower than the fathomless and dense zone of darkness, the ocean illuminates itself again and that a golden and motionless light sprouts from gigantic sponges as radiant and as yellow as suns. All types of plants and frozen beings live there submerged in that light of glacial, eternal summer: green and red sea anemones crowd themselves in broad live meadows to which transparent jellyfish that have not yet broken their ties intertwine themselves before embarking on an errant destiny through the seas; hard white coral becomes entangled in enchanted thickets where slithering fish of shadowy velvet softly open and close themselves like flowers; there are sea horses whose manes of algae scatter round them in a sluggish halo when they silently gallop, and if one lifts certain grey shells of insignificant shape, one is frequently sure to find below a little mermaid crying.

I know about an underwater volcano in constant eruption; its crater boils indefatigably day and night and it blows thick bubbles of silvery lava toward the surface of the waters.

I know that during the low-tide, painted beds of delicate anemones remain uncovered on the reefs, and I commiserate with the one who smells that ardent carpet that devours.

I know about gulfs replete with eternal foam where the west winds slowly drag their innumerable rainbow tails.

There is a pure white and nude drowned woman that all of the fishermen of the coast vainly try to catch in their nets...but perhaps she is nothing more than an enraptured sea gull that the Pacific currents drag back and forth.

I am familiar with hidden roads, terrestrial channels where the ocean filters the tides, in order to climb up to the pupils of certain women who suddenly look at us with deeply green eyes.

I know that the ships that have fallen down the ladder of a whirlwind continue travelling centuries below in between submerged reefs; that their masts entangle infuriated octopi and that their holds harbor starfish.

All this I know about the sea.

I know from the earth, that whoever removes the bark from certain trees will find sleeping and adhering to the trunk, extraordinary dusty butterflies that the first ray of light pierces and destroys like an implacable, irreverent pin.

I remember and I see an autumn park. In its wide avenues the leaves pile up and decay, and below them palpitate timid moss colored frogs that wear a golden crown on their heads. No one knows it, but the truth is that all frogs are princes.

I fear "la gallina ciega"* with the immeasurable fright of a child. "La gallina ciega" is smoke colored, and she lives cast below the thickets, like a miserable pile of ashes. She doesn't have legs to walk, nor eyes to see; but she usually flies away on certain nights with short and thick wings. No one knows where she goes, no one knows from where she returns, at dawn, stained in blood that isn't her own.

---

*La gallina ciega is more commonly identified with the childhood game of "blind man's bluff." Here, Bombal creates a legend about the figure of an actual blind hen and refers to her in mysterious and somewhat macabre terms.

I am familiar with a distant southern jungle in whose muddy ground opens a hole narrow and so deep that if you lie face downwards upon the earth and you look, you will encounter as far as the eye can see, something like a cloud of golden dust that vertiginously turns.

But nothing is more unforseen than the birth of wine. Because it isn't true that wine is born under the sky and within the dark grape of water and sun. The birth of wine is tenebrous and slow; I know a lot about that furtive assassin's growth. Only after the doors of the cold wine cellar are closed and after the spiders have spread out their first curtains, is when the wine decides to grow in the depths of the large, hermetically closed barrels. Like the tides, wine suffers from the taciturn influence of the moon that now incites it to retreat, now helps it to flow back. And this is how it is born and grows in the darkness and the silence of its winter.

I can tell something more about the earth. I know about a deserted region where a village has remained buried in the dunes, the only thing emerging is the peak of the tower of the church. During stormy nights every lightning rod moves recklessly over the solitary arrow, erect in the middle of the plain, coiling around her, whistling, in order to later sink into the sand. And they say that then, the missing tower shakes from top to bottom and a subterranean toll of bells is heard resonating.

The sky, on the other hand, does not have even one small and tender secret. Implacable, it completely unfurls its terrifying map above us.

I would like to believe that I have my star, the one that I see break through first and shine an instant only for me everyday at dusk, and that in that star not only my steps but also my laughter and my voice have an echo. But, alas, I know too well that there cannot be life of any kind there where the atoms change their form millions of times per second and where no pair of atoms can remain united.

It even makes me afraid to name the sun. It is so powerful! If they were to cut us off from its radiation, the course of the rivers would immediately stop.

I barely dare to speak about a condor that the winds pushed beyond the terrestrial atmosphere and that, still alive, has been falling in infinite space for an uncountable number of years.

Perhaps the sudden fall of shooting stars responds to a foreseen call from eternity that hurls them in order to form particular geometric figures, made of glittering stars inlaid in a remote corner of the sky. Perhaps.

No, I don't want, I don't want to talk about the sky any more, because I fear it, and I fear the dreams with which it frequently enters into my nights. Then, it extends a sidereal ladder to me through which I climb toward the shining dome. The moon stops being a pallid disk stuck in the firmament in order to become a scarlet ball that rolls through space in solitude. The stars grow larger in a blinking of rays, the milky way approaches and pours out its wave of fire. And, second by second, I am closer to the edge of that burning precipice.

No, I prefer to imagine a diurnal sky with roaming castles of clouds in whose floating rooms flutter the dry leaves of a terrestrial autumn and the kites that the sons of men lost, playing.

Translated by Celeste Kostopulos-Cooperman

Genealogies

Margo Glantz

"A tall cossack and a short one passed by our house, with their hands covered in blood, and my mother, crying her eyes out, washed their hands in a bowl." My father's mother wore those broad skirts that we all know now, after reading or seeing *The Tin Drum*: she hid my two aunts, Jane and Myra, girls of sixteen and seventeen, under them.

"I was almost out of my mind, I walked (I was only a boy), I ran from one place to another and crossed the town over the little bridge that led to the baths and I tried to find shelter in my uncle Kalmen's house, he was my father's brother. It was 1917. I went into my uncle's house and I almost went mad, my uncle had a long curly red beard, all crimson with blood, and he was sitting with the blood pouring down and his eyes open. The fear of death still hadn't left him, perhaps he was still even breathing! Beside him, wrapped in a sheet were all the household utensils, everything made of silver or copper, the Sabbath candlesticks, the samovar. I was scared stiff, I had no idea what to do, I just ran out of the village like a madman. The pogrom lasted several days, I went out into the country and I found an abandoned well, deep, but with no water in it, and I clung to the rungs and spent several days down there. When I heard that everything had calmed down, I came out. Before that, I could hear the terrible cries of the girls and children."

It all happened so fast that one pogrom piled up on top of another.

"In those troubled times different groups were chasing one another and as they went through towns and villages they sacked everything in their path."

It all sounds so familiar. It's like those revolts that our nineteenth century novelists wrote about and like what you read in novels about the Mexican Revolution, the revolts and the levies, the confusion, the sacking of towns and villages, the deaths.

"The Bolsheviks came back and we had some of the short rifles left by the bandits and some of the horses too; only the reservists who'd been in the World War knew how to defend themselves, the rest of us were saved by a miracle. Many of the bandits were peasants who knew us, and as they were stealing they preferred to kill so that they couldn't be denounced."

Yasha hid in the house of a muzhik, a friend of his grandfather's, Sasha Ribak "with an enormous moustache, like the poet Sevshenko" (the great popular poet of the Ukraine). My father stayed hiding in a corncrib, breathing through a hole, even when bandits stuck their bayonets into it. Ribak took him food and water and let him out when things calmed down a little. As soon as things started up again, back my father went to his hideout.

"General Budiony's Bolshevik cossacks arrived. When things were a bit calmer, I came out. When it was dangerous I went back into hiding again. I remember Sasha well; he was very good. I wrote a poem about all that, in 1920, in Russia."

"And what about your mother and your sisters, how were they saved?"

"We survived by chance, by luck. My mother and my sisters hid in the top of the house, where there was a loft used as a storeroom, in the space under the rafter. As the groups were all chasing each other, they hardly had time to look, and they sacked and killed everything they found in their way. My mother was saved that first time because she washed the cossacks' hands."

*   *   *

My grandmother and two aunts were given permission to leave Russia around 1923 to rejoin their family in *America, America* (the title of the famous film by Elia Kazan). My father was doing his military service and had to stay in the Soviet Union.

"Your mother was afraid that I'd get lost in the revolution. I was very impulsive, it was a dangerous situation and the revolution didn't tolerate people who were impulsive. What the revolution demanded was total commitment from each individual, and those who tried to see things their own way were put on the list of counter-revolutionaries. Well, I was pretty well done for, as you can imagine, being a gabby Jew. And later on they arrested me."

"Why did they arrest you?"

"They arrested me for. . .you see, I was marked down in the revolution as a man with nationalist deviationist tendencies."

My grandmother and my aunts stayed on in Russia for another year after being granted permission to leave, because my grandmother was afraid she might never see her son again. But in the end they travelled to Turkey and then they couldn't go any further because the North Americans had restricted their immigration quotas and only the mother was eligible to enter the United States. However, my father was also granted permission to leave, though afterwards he went to a protest meeting about unfair practices that prevented people from obtaining work. One of the men who had been refused work threw himself out of a fourth floor window as a protest, then the police arrived and put most of the protesters in jail, including my father.

At his point in the story a friend of the family turns up, a pro-Soviet Jew who had left Russia round 1924 and emigrated to Cuba in 1928, from where he had been chased out by Machado's henchmen because of his militancy. He has brought some Soviet journals sent him from New York, worth 123.50 pesos.

"They used to reach me quickly direct from Moscow. They only cost 17.50 pesos then, but you have to pay a full year's subscription."

"When did you leave Russia?"

"My family left first. My father went to the United States in 1912. He left my mother in Russia with the children. In 1914 he sent us tickets and we were due to leave on the 19th of August and the First World War broke out on the 29th. My father went back to Russia in 1922, but he couldn't settle, because he was a businessman and they accused him of being a bourgeois, so in 1923 he went to New York with his other two brothers. I went to Cuba in 1924, but then they brought in new regulations about immigration quotas so I couldn't go on to the United States."

"That's what happened to us too," says Yankl.

"I went on to Mexico later, because otherwise I'd have ended up drowned in the bay at Havana sooner or later."

His friend leaves, and my father comments:

"He stayed you know, he's one of the very few who stayed on the left."

He insists on recalling that meeting where a worker threw himself down from the fourth floor. I remember something similar in one of Wajda's films.

"Then the riot started," interrupts Mother. "The police were there and they started taking workers away. They took your father along with a friend of his, a journalist who was about forty. Your father didn't turn up and I was worried and I started looking for him round the police stations. I asked different policemen about him and nobody knew anything. I said to one of them, you've got your people all over the place, don't you know or can't you tell me? He told me he couldn't say anything. It was a Thursday. On Saturday a lady came to see me. I was playing the piano and she asked me if I was Glantz's fiancee. I was surprised, but I said yes. 'I've brought you a message from your fiancee that my husband gave me, because both of them have been arrested.'"

*   *   *

"I travelled third class, that is, your father and I did. And I couldn't eat anything, because the food was so awful, even though there were times when we went hungry. There was a very bright woman who got on well with the zeil meister and she used to give us herring with vinegar and onions, and that was a real treat. I sold everything in Moscow because I was going to Cuba and Russian clothes wouldn't be any use over there. I had some very smart grey suede shoes which were open down the front and a pair of stockings that I had to darn every day. In Holland we got some money from Uncle Ellis and I bought two dresses, a black crepe one which was very smart and one in lovely soft green wool."

It's raining, San Miguel Regla is really beautiful, with its gentle countryside and all the trees, the house with its slender columns, that huge, friendly hacienda which I almost like better than Marienbad, a place I've only ever seen on film, except that I'm a bit of a snob and it seems rather more exotic to me, as the mother of my Colombian friend said, when we were in Paris and she was talking about American clothes:

"They're so nice, they look so foreign!"

Mother goes on talking: "Your father wasn't worried, in the daytime we stayed under cover and at night we slept in our cabin. (And to think that so much love can actually wear itself out!)

"There was a very interesting man travelling with us, a very strange man, he spoke Russian but I think he was born in Poland. We called him Miloshka, which means 'favorite'. He disappeared when we got here" she sighs, then continues: "You know, when we came to Mexico I didn't know how to use earthenware pots, so at first I boiled milk in a pan a lot, and now I can't stand blenders, I prefer to mash things in an old Mexican earthenware bowl. You can get used to anything, that's for sure. Though I still don't know where I really am."

"What do you mean?"

"I still don't know if I'm on my own or what. I don't want to send your father's books because it'll make the place seem so empty."

"You should send his books, and his papers so they can be put in order and catalogued. I think it's the right thing to do; they'll be very useful for people who are trying to write the history of the Mexican Jewish community."

The ground is wet. We have been sitting in a little garden, surrounded by cloistered arches, on antique style leather chairs, like the rest of the hacienda, like the bedrooms. Later we sit around the fireplace. The cleaning woman says softly "there's a bit of watery sunshine." Everything is so peaceful, so lovely, so melancholy. I've eaten so much I can hardly move. I go out for a long walk, through the trees, past the pools, the remains of the old metal smelting furnace, and memories flood back with every step, memories of the former owner, the Marquis of Guadalupe, Count of Regla, my mother's memories.

"That's how I learned to make strudel."

"When did you learn that? Did you learn it at home? Did your mother teach you?"

"Yes, I learned quite a lot from her in Russia. In Tacuba street, number 15, there was a restaurant and there was a Russian man who had emigrated there recently and he was chief cook, and I don't know how it came about, but I think I said to him that you could make strudel in the little coal burning ovens, the portable ones, with two chimney vents and two openings, and they were making strudels and I made one and he liked it a lot. . ."

We go in because it is starting to rain.

"He said to me: 'Such a lovely young woman with all sorts of talents and she's interested in strudel.' And I just got on and made it, and I don't even remember how much he paid me. We used to go to the club in the evenings. . ."

"You and strudel man?"

"No, me and your father. We used to see Mr. Perkis there, and Dr. King and Katzenelson. Everybody changed their names. First they were living in the United States and then when the First World War broke out they went to Mexico to start again, and they founded the Young Men's Hebrew Association."

"With an English name?"

"Yes, English because they'd just come from the United States, you see. they looked after us, in a way. Dr. King used to give your father dental products, I've told you that already. And our father used to teach Hebrew at first to some of the children, our friends' children when they were preparing for their barmitzvahs. Some people were very kind, and we were very grateful to people too. Horacio Minich's father, for example, taught natural sciences in the Yiddish school, but since I didn't know any Yiddish I couldn't even teach things I knew about."

"So what did you know about?"

"Lots of things, I was always learning, I never seemed to stop. Playing the piano, science, art, even singing. But I ended up having to make strudel. That's the way it is. We brought lots of books instead of clothing, we had a basket of books that weighed 60 kilos. They were very important books and important people used to ask to borrow them and most of them we never set eyes on again. That's the way it is."

"Do you still have any of those books?"

"Oh yes, there are a few left but I'm going to send them to Israel. There was a group of non-Jewish Russians here too, some very nice people, they were quite old, well, at least they seemed quite old to me."

"How old were they?"

"I don't know, but they were a lot older than we were. They lived in Xochimilco, which was a big place in those days, very beautiful with a lot of flowers everywhere and boats covered with greenery. They had a herb garden, they were typical Russians, very refined, honest, special people. There were some others who were former nobility. What were their names? How could I forget? Oh, yes, they were called Sokolov."

"Who were? The ones with the herb garden or the others?"

"No, the other ones, the nobility, were much younger. I don't remember what the others were called, but they had a little house in Xochimilco, it wasn't much more than a hut. They made us a typical Russian meal, they were so pleased to be able to speak Russian with someone."

"Anything else, Mother?"

"Oh, Margo, it all happened fifty years ago, Every night we used to go to the club, it didn't matter if you were on the right or the left, nobody bothered. Then Abrams came, and he was an anarchist, as real leftist. It didn't matter what we did during the daytime to earn a living, because in the evenings we all went to the club."

"Why didn't it matter what you did in the daytime?"

"Well, we sold bread, or I don't know, some people were peddlers, street traders during the daytime, but in the evening we all came together for something better. There were all sorts of people, some as young as 14 or 15. You never knew them, maybe you did or maybe you didn't, but we all had to use Yiddish because we couldn't manage any other way. Some of them had come from Poland and some from Russia and some came from tiny little villages where they spoke a sort of Yiddish, and some even came from the United States and goodness knows what sort of English they could speak. So we all had to learn Yiddish, and when I started I couldn't understand anything because there were so many dialects, from Warsaw and Lithuania and Rumania and Lestonia and little Polish villages. I couldn't understand a word and then I started to learn gradually. Your father used to read to me, he was in bed a lot because he had trouble with his lungs and sometimes he used to cough up blood, and then he had to lie down because that frightened him. Your father used to read me Yiddish books, he used to translate them into Russian and that's how I learned. I knew the alphabet because when I was a little girl I'd been taught that before I went on to high school."

"Didn't your mother speak Yiddish?"

"Of course she did, but she spoke a Ukrainian dialect, which was completely different. Later on all sorts of very well educated young people used to come to our house. . ."

"Later on when?"

"In Russia. Before I went to high school. They used to come to Odessa from their little villages to study and take important exams. I remember before the First World War there was one of those students living in our house, a Zionist, who knew Hebrew perfectly. We put him up and fed him and he used to give us Hebrew lessons. He gave lessons to uncle Volodia, but I don't remember if

Ilusha and I did any. That's how I learned the alphabet. He went to Israel later. Your uncle Volodia told me he went on to become Minister of Finance."

"In Israel?"

"Yes, in Israel. Uncle Volodia could remember his name, but I can't. I learned the alphabet and when I learned some Yiddish I wrote a letter to my parents once, just a few words. My mother wrote back in a terrible state because I'd suddenly written to her in Yiddish and she didn't think it could be me, she thought I must be dead, so then I wrote back again to her in Russian and calmed things down. That's what it's like when your children leave home..."

I come back to where I once was. I go through the park, past the pools, and everything is damp, mildewed. It is slippery underfoot. There are flowers everywhere. I go over to a prickly pear tree and try to pluck some fruit. The pear defends itself and sticks its spikes in me. I go back to my room to try and pull out the prickles with a pair of tweezers from my arms, my cheeks, and the side of my mouth, my hands and my fingers. My father died, early in the morning of January 2, 1982.

*   *   *

Living with someone probably means losing part of your own identity. Living with someone contaminates; my father alters my mother's childhood and she loses her patience listening to some accounts of my father's childhood. Once we had all gone to the cemetery on the first anniversary of my uncle's death and Lucia recalled the attempted pogrom that my father had experienced. So I asked him to tell me what had happened to him:

"I was working in the Jewish Charity Association at 21 Gante Street, on the corner of Venustiano Carranza that used to be called Capuchinas, and your mother had her shop called Lisette on 16th September Street, number 29, selling ladies' bags and gloves. I came out of the charity place and there was a big meeting underway (it was in January, 1939). I was on my way to the shop when I met a young man called Salas, he knew who I was, he'd been a student in Germany and spoke very good German. He came toward me with two other lads and he yelled 'Death to the Jews. Jews out of Mexico!' and I had a willow stick with me, and I broke it over his head and it split into three. He grabbed it out of my hand and tried to push me in front of a tram, but I held onto a lamp-post and wouldn't let go. I don't know how I managed to break free and run to the shop, which was shut, though the steel door still wasn't down.

"The police came right away, I don't remember how many there were, there could have been fifty or a hundred, and Siqueiros' brother; if he hadn't been there I'd have been killed. He said to me: 'They'll have to get me before they get you, Jacobo,' and he stretched both arms out wide. He was a giant of a man. They had a truck outside full of stones and they were throwing them at the shop and they smashed the shop window and took everything they could get. I don't know how I got out of there."

"Where was mother?"

"She'd got out with the assistant. There were stones flying all over the place. I didn't know where to hide, because everywhere I went there were more stones. I thought I'd never get out of there, I thought I was done for, there was nothing I could do. There were so many people outside and so many stones and I was covered in blood. There was a man called Osorio outside, a Cuban that I knew quite well, and he stood up on a platform and made a Hitler-type speech, and even though he knew me he spoke against me and against Jews in general. When they ran out of stones, they went to San Juan de Letran where your uncle Mendel had his drinks stand and they came back with great chunks of ice which they started throwing at me, and a massive lump of ice hit me on the head and that was a sign from God, because the ice saved me. I was bleeding heavily, because I'd been hit on the head, but that ice was a sign from God, I wouldn't have survived without the ice."

"Where were we?"

"You were all very little, I don't think you ever saw any of that.

General Montes appeared later and he put his cloak round me and said, 'Don't cry Jew, I'm here to save you.' "

Translated by Susan Bassnett

Destinations

"Good Evening, Agatha"

Yolanda Bedregal

After a pale day, which is how the days in the country are, I closed the window of the little room. The nostalgic smell of the papers and memories I was burning in the brazier still hung in the air. A piece of the smoky late afternoon was encased by the whitewashed walls. It was a Saturday, one of those that seems to have no Monday. I could now give myself over to my humble kind of joy: to converse in silence with my only treasure, my grandparents' icon. This was a polychromed image carved from the wood of an orange tree. A rigid blue mantle opened fan-like from the head to the coarse red wool of the indigenous cloth. The tiny hands, crossed on her breast, supported a barely perceptible dove and a disproportionately small baby. . .I had a child, too, once. He isn't alive any more; he died in the hospital. And his father, where might he be? He was a being as sad and gray as the landscape in which we met. Did he love me? Perhaps. We came together the way two lone shrubs join in the pampa. How can there be two human beings as forsaken as he and I were! Our encounter was sweet, bitter and brief. The little bit accumulated there became a truncated chapter, like fragments of ruins that speak, promise things that once were and never will be again, that sleep in the future of things remembered.

But I was going to tell what happened that late afternoon, while I spoke with the orangewood Madonna. I told myself that everything was like that image. There was nothing in the world that was not as she was. Earth, wood, flesh or spirit: noble material. The work of God, of Nature or of man. I sensed that everything has a limit in space and in time, encircled by a line, sinuous or smooth, which finally doubles back upon itself. This outline grazes what is unending, eternal. When signatures destruct they link up with that which is infinite. When wood turns to dust, my eyes, too, will have been transformed into a substance capable of contemplating this and a mysterious bond, barely stirring in memory, would again unite us in another sphere.

Sensing this, I prayed a beadless mental rosary. I lit a candle and let my hands, like two rugged cactus blooms, rest on the table. My hands have a strange property. Normally long, sinewy and bony, love transfigures them: the veins slowly tend to disappear like rivers in sand, the skin becomes warm like a tree in the sun, the nails acquire a lustre as of underwater mother-of-pearl, the fingers forget needle and coal. At such times my hands leave their sleeves and become detached, as though bloodlessly severed. By themselves they have a life different from my own; they no longer belong to me; I would be incapable even of lifting them. I contemplate them, thus abandoned...But to return to what happened that afternoon. The tongue of the candle flickered a secret language that caused things to quiver slightly. The walls drew back, the table, enlarged by the shadow, trembled. The icon bent toward my skirt or fled out the half-closed window.

Suddenly, without warning, the door opens. A man enters, a man like any other with his invisible I, unassailable and with a suit that conceals him. As with all men, has he any idea of what he is or what he wants? The years have fused onto him a mask of frustrated minutes, society has imposed on him his facade and treacherous attitudes; the authorities have added on papers in his

pockets, tags on his lapel. If he did not need documents to identify him, he would be unmistakable. The possession of a passport,
a document of identification, rental receipts, tax vouchers, a wal-
let, keys, makes everyone the same, even though the police main-
tain the contrary.

As though the gloom had cleansed him of falsehood and he were
again himself, the pilgrim regards me with eternal eyes and, with
a voice that is timeless, definitive and clean, says, "Good evening,
Agatha."

Agatha...Who told him? When I was going to have my child,
in the event that it would be a girl I was going to name her Agatha.
But no one knew that. How did it occur to him to call me that?
My name is so different.

I answer him calmly from my seat. "Good evening."

On some other occasion, perhaps startled, I ask him who he
is, why he came, what he wants, all those inquisitive sentences we
expend and by means of which we make strangers even more alien.
But after that greeting everything seemed natural to me. My faded
life, detached from everyone, was perhaps just like his own. What
can we discover about a human being if with each superficial word
we deepen the abyss? One comes to the earth, one suffers, loves,
struggles, waits. And? We're all the same. He could have said to
me, "My name is Christopher, I am a carpenter, I have come to
offer you this frame."

At heart it would be just as false as any other explanation.

Perhaps he was alone, filled with anxiety or fatigue, saw a light
through the crack, felt the desire to enter the first available doorway, sit down in the first vacant easy chair and bestow his imper-
sonal presence the same way one looks out at the sea or at the
high plateau, or as one cries for no reason, just like that, just because.
We have so many impulses that are stifled by cowardice. I had them,
too, simple, generous, human: to hug the ragged child that is playing in the mud, to kiss the forehead of the blind beggar, to take
care of the neighbor's children for her. Other absurd but pure
desires: that a bird might come to perch on my shoulder, that an
unknown man like a lifelong lover might take me to bed and allow

me to sleep upon his pillow without anguish, without desire, without hurry. All of them longings that were unfulfilled, hidden behind a wall of distrust.

Well, then. The visitor stopped the air from the street with his body. He shut the rickety pane behind him and, without necessary permission, sat down at the foot of the cot with his silence and his invisible burden. He rested his head on the cross of his forearms propped up on the rail.

I refused to look at him so as not to spoil the brief eternity of that human sculpture.

My hands rejoined my body. From a distance I caressed the arch of his shoulder. When he raised his head I asked if I could offer him my coffee. He gestured his refusal. Later, without breaking his intimate wholeness, he took out a cigarette; he rolled it slowly in his fingers. He doesn't have a light—I thought—and indicated the kitchen area to him. Without hesitation he went to the shelf, to the exact place where the matches are kept.

A fleeting star shone in the hollow of his hands. With the tenuous brightness the icon lit up. This timeless minute converged on it.

The man smoked, at first avidly and then with the solemn slowness which we give to final gestures. Afterwards I heard the light crackle of paper being unfolded. I was unwilling to break with a glance the atmosphere which the stranger had created, but I sensed that he was crumpling a letter and hiding it. He took a deep breath, got up and said once more, "Good evening, Agatha."

When he left the room, a draft bent the tongue of the candle. Nothing has happened. A man came into my room. He smoked a cigarette, read a letter and left, without asking for anything. He has given me something of which he is unaware. Something inexpressible has remained, surrounding his absence.

This unexpected visit has been a blessing. I now know that someone can exist in this world who may arrive without knocking, who can be here without having left and who on leaving can say to me:

"Good evening, Agatha."

Translated by Nina M. Scott

An Avid One in Extremis

Hilda Hilst

for Lygia and Paulo Emilio

Spit in your face, a slap, a punch, anything better than the word, KleinKu, I call you that, name with the sonority of the language of poets and beasts, the act always better and not like me myself the thought-leap to explain myself through minimal you. I'm not dying KleinKu. I tried to explain the same thing to another one, stupid like you, named Koyo and built stockades looking for my nail, stockades around nothing, because for all that you raise up, never, closed like I am in this braided mat, neither Koyo nor KleinKu would have the visor, the perforating eye for the smallest of me. I'm not dying. Perfection is death, one of you AH discovered and said Perfection is death, wouldn't this be the greatest proof of immortality? Koyo and KleinKu locked you up, insane asylum, and this AH up against the wall can't give speeches in the congresses, senates, it would be the same, madmen on the inside, on the outside, all KleinKus repeating that I'm dead when this would be the inexpressible but the most significant of all my acts. I want to die, a single marble slab over the I whole, I'd rather the mat, that which never within your reach, not even with eyes closed,

KleinKu understand, I'm in agony but I'm not going to die, deteri-
orated, shapeless, from here on pus and dust accumulating, I should
live in silence, but the one of me in silence runs to you, expresses
itself in acts, and what acts those of yours, savagery and arrogance
in all of them, I must ask that you hurry, finish, you have the means,
more powerful than Nagasaki and Hiroshima, and there's a hunger in you too marvelous for your name, and isn't it that all your
hungers fit in your despicable hole? I don't know how one dies,
and I didn't know that thinking me would expel concept and dung-
hill, I look at you in a sobbing separating of distances, I look at
me and in the body I search for the tiniest point from where I
can extract an all new, death, if I could remake myself in death,
I kneel twisted down before myself, that the divine I find the road
to Nothingness and on the way not try again to give form to appearances, the I full of emotion wanted to translate itself into works,
thought Man to inhabit the Earth and it was as if one had thought
sordidness, fossilized faces, that Nothingness should meet me once
again, thought me Nothingness, because for an instant it intended
to give form to the Nothingness-Not Being, ah, KleinKu, I say it
again, I'd rather the spit the punch the slap, anything would be
better than the word, and if I had cornets I could use them like
this one of me, fortunate Mahler, if I had cornets, the ones post-
riders use, oh if I only had them, I would extract the most painful
sound for your impaired hearing, if I had words like those of me
Jeshua had them, some mine incendiary, but for KleinKu it was
as if I had never committed them, if the many in me could ham-
mer your substance, once again molded, a new metaplasm, two
hearts-head for the man, acting in complete communion, KleinKu
added on in some easts, torn from the south, it would have been
better to have consumed the idea-man as soon as it was expelled,
act the way I was taught by mine own, monks-cartridges volatiliz-
ing the word at its source, KleinKu thinking yes but incandescent
in the same moment returning to its root. Now black elbows braced
in my softnesses, I look at the absurd: you. Dear little mother, I
GrosseKu, also baptized by men with esoteric names, Pneuma, the
All-One, the No-Name, dear little mother I want your hand in

mine, and Gide in an endless to my ear: "I want to die in desperation." Maybe that way I'll be able, maybe that way I learn to die.

Translated by Dawn Jordan

Natural Theology

Hilda Hilst

The future's face he didn't see. Life, a gross imitation of noth-ing. So he thought about hollows of face, blindness, corroded hands, and feet, everything would be eaten by the salt, stretched out whiteness of the condemned, damned saltiness, infernal saltbed, he thought glasses gloves galoshes, thought about selling that which, all Tio sunk in brilliance, beef jerky was he, dried, salted, stretched, and the meat-face of the future where was it? He dreamed himself sweetened, cane syrup body, betterment if only he could buy the things, sell something Tio. What? In the city there are people who even buy shit in packages, if you only had a conch or oyster, ah, but your foot would never stand the whole day in the saltbed and then again at night, at the edge of the salty water, in the crevice of the rock, on the jags where the oysters used to live. He entered the house. Dryness, emptihood, from the corner she peered at him and gnawed some hard ones in the wetness of her mouth, no, she wasn't a rat, she was everything Tio owned, peering again at her son's strange acts, Tio soaking some rags, filling his hands with ashes, if I rub you right you'll whiten a little and be beautiful, I'll sell you there, and someday buy you back, softness on the tongue spoke in pauses, no hooks, I'll sell you, now the back, turn around, now you clean your belly, I'll turn around and you clean your privates, while you clean your bottom I'll get a handful of raspberries, that's enough, let's carefully spread this red mass over your face, on the cheeks, the lips, stand up straighter so you hide your hump, glasses gloves galoshes, that's all I need, if they buy anything down there in the city they should buy you, later I'll come for you, and a few dustings off, primps, a few whisps of breath on the wrinkled face, hair, giving the old lady a turn, examining her as only an expert in mothers would, dreamed-of buyer, Tio tied to his back with some old rope everything he owned, mute, small, delicate, a little speck of a mother, and smiled a lot while he walked.

Translated by Dawn Jordan

Destination

Patricia Bins

Have all the words been spoken?
What path is clear, if you hold me
bound; torn between thought and action,
in futile restraint? Robbed of the
smallest hope, bereft of all I ever
expected, on which side am I? Is this
a dream, a voyage, or some hallucination?
Yet here I remain and this vast expanse
invites exploration, full of clouds and
wild spaces, birds that neither respond nor
question but pass, attentive to the fleeting
moments of plenitude and incomprehension.
                                    —Marly de Oliveira

Sometimes we aimlessly discussed ways and means of doing
things, simply to kill time while waiting for death. We spoke without waiting for the silence that comes between the word and its
utterance, and we failed to hear the spaces between the lines. We

only knew what was obvious: that we were two distinct beings.

Meanwhile, we had to carry on, to feign our reality, to live and relive the various roles assigned to us, or that we demanded of ourselves.

Hence the shallow bid for power, conducted through games, intricate games without love or memory.

Why did we fail to love each other? Obviously, it was the biblical tale retold, envy gnawing away our very heart. It did not even occur to us that we would never attain perfection if tainted by rancor.

Immersed in the hallucination of power, fantasy served as consolation. Ah, base glory, corrupt divinity, foolish pride, the dramas of lust, vanity, greed, wrath, sloth, and, above all, avarice. Neither of us was prepared to make even a kind gesture. We held back, as if afraid of squandering our feelings.

And then the daily losses: those facile transformations in order to survive within the commonplace. No sign of the divine territory, yet within our reach, should we so desire.

Until we should decide to cross the bridge. A new challenge within the same mediocre limits: was this our intention? Or was there something beckoning us beyond errors that systematically conditioned our existence?

The night was tranquil. There were stars and the moonlight cast its light over the path we followed, unaware of our destiny. Familiar landscapes disappeared from sight and others of exceptional beauty were revealed to us. We laughed to the wind, unaccustomed to the freedom of being, for however briefly, whole and entire.

The tang of the sea was more potent than any other aroma, announcing the next phase into which we were about to plunge. Everything remained uncertain, except for those aromas that came and went, the ebbs and flows of tides we could only intuit.

We divined the sands and an aurora.

At last we saw the house as in a dream.

Someone opened the door to us, and there were other doors along lengthy corridors that we might be able to open later. We were assailed by the smell of mustiness as we entered the house, only to discover once inside that the mirrors were covered in haze. Yet they reflected our faces, our unknown bodies, our questing souls.

By candlelight we recognized the inhabitants of the earth: cats followed by dogs came to sniff. Then we heard the songs of birds.

A man received us, as if we were expected. His smiling wife betrayed no surprise to find us wearing masks: she appeared to be saying that they were essential for survival from that previous phase. In silence, because words would have been superfluous, and in the forbidding presence of love, we greeted each other.

Yawns announced sleep without soporifics. We returned to the comfort of forgotten sensibilities, free from capital sins. Only the original sin, the option of being or not being. A dream about something dreamed?

In the morning, the realization that there really are no barriers when we transcend the limits of mediocrity. God effortlessly assumed. And now to escape, to relish our destiny once aware of our humanity. Moist sands underfoot, steps heard in the distance, in silence. Our own steps perhaps?—rapid and joyful.

Translated by Giovanni Pontiero

I Love My Husband

Nelida Piñon

I love my husband. From morning to night. Scarcely awake, I
offer him coffee. He sighs, exhausted by his usual poor night's sleep,
and begins to shave. I knock on his door three times, lest his coffee get cold. He grunts in anger and I clamor in distress. I don't
want my effort confused with a cold liquid that he will consume
just as he consumes me twice a week, especially on Saturdays.

Afterwards, I fix the knot of his tie and he protests because I
have fixed merely the smallest part of his life. I laugh so he can
go off more calmly, ready to face life outside and bring an always
warm and bountiful loaf of bread back to our living room.

He says that I'm demanding, that I stay home to wash dishes,
go shopping, and on top of that, complain about life. Meanwhile,
he builds his world with little bricks, and though some of these
walls topple to the ground, his friends compliment him on his effort
at creating brickyards, all solid and visible, from clay.

They salute me, too, for nourishing a man who dreams of mansions, shanties, and huts, and so makes the nation progress. And
that is why I am the shadow of the man whom everyone says I

love. I let the sun enter the house, to brighten up the objects bought with our joint effort. Even so, he never compliments me on the luminescent objects. To the contrary, through his certainty about my love, he proclaims that I do nothing but consume the money that he gathers together in the summer. Then I ask him to understand my nostalgia for the terrain formerly worked by women; he furrows his brow as though I were proposing a theory that disgraces the family and the definitive deed to our apartment.

What more do you want, woman? Isn't it enough for you that we married with community property? And while he was saying that I was part of his future, one that only he, however, had the right to build, I noticed that the man's generosity qualified me to be only the mistress of a past whose rules were dictated in shared intimacy.

I began to think longingly about how wonderful it would be to live only in the past, before this preterit time was dictated for us by the man we say we love. He applauded my scheme. Within the house, in the oven that was the hearth, it would be easy to nourish the past with herbs and oatmeal so that he could calmly manage the future. He definitely couldn't preoccupy himself with the uterus of my womb, which must belong to him in such a way that he wouldn't need to smell my sex to discover who else, besides him, had been there, had knocked at the door, had scratched inscriptions and dates onto its walls.

My son must be only mine, he confessed to his friends on the Saturday of the month that we entertained. And a woman must be only mine and not even her own. The idea that I couldn't belong to myself, touch my sex to purge it of excesses, provoked the first shock to the fantasy about the past in which I had been immersed until then. So the man, as well as having shipwrecked me in the past while he felt free to live the life to which only he had access, also needed to bind my hands, so my hands wouldn't feel the softness of my own skin. Would this softness perhaps tell me in a low voice that there was other skin equally sweet and private, covered with velvety fuzz, and that one could lick its salt with the tongue's help?

I looked at my fingers, revolted by the long, magenta-painted nails. Nails of a tiger that strengthened my identity and grunted about the truth of my sexuality. I caressed my body. I thought, Am I a woman only through my long claws, and by clothing them with gold, silver, the sudden rush of blood of an animal slaughtered in the woods? Or because the man adorns me in such a way that when I remove this warpaint from my face he is surprised by a visage he doesn't recognize, which he covered with mystery so he wouldn't have me whole?

Suddenly, the mirror seemed to me the symbol of a defeat, which the man brought home and which made me become pretty. Isn't it true that I love you, husband? I asked him while he was reading the newspapers to keep himself informed, and I was sweeping up the letters of print spit out on the floor as soon as he assimilated the news. He said, Let me go on, woman. How can you expect me to talk about love when they're discussing the economic alternatives for a country in which the men need to work twice as hard as slaves to support the women?

Then I said to him, If you don't want to discuss love, which, after all, could perfectly well be far from here, or behind the furniture where I sometimes hide the dust after I sweep the house, what if after so many years I were to mention the future as though it were a kind of dessert?

He put the newspaper aside and insisted that I repeat what I had said. I spoke of the word 'future' cautiously, not wanting to wound him, but I no longer refrained from an African adventure recently-initiated at that very moment. Followed by a retinue oiled with sweat and anxiety, I was slaughtering the wild boars, immersing my canines in their warm jugulars, while Clark Gable, attracted by my scent and that of the animal in convulsions, was begging for my love on bended knee. Made voracious by the effort, I gulped river water, perhaps in search of the fever in my innards which I didn't know how to arouse. My burning skin, the delirium, and the words that sullied my lips for the first time, as I blushed with pleasure and modesty, while the witch doctor saved my life with his ritual and the abundant hair on his chest. Health in my fingers, the breath of life seemed to exhale from my mouth, and then I left Clark Gable tied in a tree, slowly eaten by ants. Imitating Nayoka, I went down the river, which had almost attacked me by force; avoiding the waterfalls, I proclaimed liberty, the most ancient and myriad of inheritances, with shouts.

My husband, with the word 'future' floating before his eyes and the newspaper fallen to the floor, demanded to know: What does this repudiation of a love nest, security, tranquility, in short, our marvelous conjugal peace, mean? And do you think, husband, that conjugal peace allows itself to be bound by threads woven through guile, simply because I mentioned that word which saddens you so much that you start to cry discreetly, for your pride doesn't permit you the convulsive weeping that is set aside for me as a woman? Oh, husband, if such a word has the impact to blind you, I'll sacrifice myself once more so I won't see you suffer. Could it be that there is still time to save you, by blotting out the future now?

His glistening craters quickly absorbed the tears, he inhaled the cigarette smoke voluptuously, and he resumed reading. It would be hard to find a man like him in our building with its eighteen floors and three entrances. At the condominium meetings at which I was present, he was the only one to overcome the obstacles and forgive those who had offended him. I blamed my egoism for having thus disturbed the night of someone who deserved to recuperate for the following day's efforts.

To hide my shame, I brought him fresh coffee and chocolate cake. He allowed me to redeem myself. He spoke to me about the monthly expenses. With the company's balance sheet slightly in the red, he had to be careful about expenditures. If he could count on my cooperation, he would dismiss his partner in less than a year. I felt happy to participate in an event that would see us make progress in twelve months. Without my backing, he would never have dreamed so high. I took upon myself, from a distance, his capacity to dream. Each of my husband's dreams was maintained by me. And for that right I reimbursed life with a check that couldn't be entered in the books.

He didn't need to thank me. He had attained perfection of tender feelings in such a way that it was enough for him to remain in my company to indicate that he loved me, I was the most exquisite fruit of the earth, a tree in the center of our living room terrain, he climbed the tree, he reached the fruits, he stroked their rind, pruning the tree's excesses.

For a week I knocked on the bathroom door with just an early-morning touch. Ready to make him new coffee if the first became cold, if, forgetfully, he stood looking at himself in the mirror with the same vanity that was instilled in me from birth as soon as it was confirmed that they were dealing with yet another woman. To be a woman is to lose oneself in time, that was my mother's rule. She meant, who overcomes time better than the feminine condition? Father applauded her, concluding: Time is not the woman's aging, but rather her mystery never revealed to the world.

Just think, daughter, what is more beautiful than a life never revealed, which no one has gathered except your husband, the father of your children? Paternal teachings were always serious, he gave the luster of silver to the word 'aging.' I became convinced that in return for not fulfilling the story of woman, that biography of her own not permitted to her, she was assured youth.

Only one who lives, ages, my father said on my wedding day. And because you will live your husband's life, we guarantee you that through this act you will always be young. I didn't know how to get around the jubilation that enveloped me with the weight of a shield, and to go to his heart, surprise his sincerity. Or to thank him for a state I had not desired before, perhaps just because I was absent-minded. And that whole trophy on the very night I would be transformed into a woman. For until then they whispered to me that I was a beautiful anticipation. Different from my brother, for already at the baptismal font they had affixed to him the glorious stigmata of man, before he had slept with a woman.

They always told me that a woman's soul emerged only in bed, her sex anointed by the man. Before him, my mother hinted, our sex most resembled an oyster nourished in salt water, and therefore vague and slippery, far from the captive reality of earth. Mother liked poetry, her images were always fresh and warm.

My heart blazed on my wedding night. I yearned for the new body they had promised me, to abandon the shell that had covered me in appropriate everyday life. My husband's hands would mold me until my final days, and how could I thank him for such generosity? For this reason, perhaps, we are as happy as two creatures can be when only one of them brings to the hearth food, hope, the faith, a family's history.

He is the only one to bring me life, even though sometimes I live it a week late. Which makes no difference. I even have an advantage, because he always brings it translated. I don't have to interpret the facts, fall into error, appear to those disquieting words that end up silencing liberty. Man's words are those I must need my whole life. I don't have to assimilate a vocabulary incompatible with my destiny, capable of ruining my marriage.

Thus I proceeded to learn that my conscience, which is at the service of my happiness, is simultaneously at the service of my husband. Its duty is to cut back my excesses, nature endowed me with the desire to be shipwrecked at times, to go to the bottom of the sea in search of sponges. And for what purpose would they serve me, if not to absorb my dreams, multiply them in the bubbling silence of their labyrinths full of seawater? I want a dream that can be grasped with a strong glove and at times be transformed into a chocolate torte for him to eat with shining eyes, and we will smile together.

Ah, when I feel like a warrior, ready to take up arms and acquire a face that isn't mine, I immerse myself in golden elation, I walk on roads with no addresses, as though from me and through my effort I should conquer another country, a new language, a body that sucks up life without fear or modesty. And everything within me trembles, I look, with an appetite for which I won't be ashamed later, at those who pass. Fortunately, it's a fleeting sensation, soon I seek the help of familiar sidewalks, my life is stamped on them. The shop windows, the objects, the friendly people, my pride, finally, in everything about my house.

These bird-like actions of mine are quite unworthy, they would wound my husband's honor. Contrite, in my thoughts I ask him forgiveness, I promise him I'll avoid such temptations. He seems to pardon me from a distance, he applauds my submission to happy everyday life, which obliges us to prosper each year. I confess that this anxiety embarrasses me, I don't know how to quell it. I don't mention it except to myself. Not even conjugal vows keep me in rare moments from shipwrecking in dream. Those vows that make my body blush but have not marked my life in such a way that I can point out the wrinkles that have come to me through their impetus.

I've never mentioned these short, dangerous gallops to my husband. He couldn't support the weight of that confession. Or if I told him that on those afternoons I think about working outside the home, to pay for odds and ends with my own money. Obviously this madness seizes me precisely because of my free time. I am princess of the house, he sometimes tells me, and with reason. Therefore, nothing should distance me from the happiness in which I am forever submerged.

I can't complain. Every day my husband contradicts the version in the mirror. I look at myself in it and he insists that I perceive myself wrongly. I am not, in truth, the shadows, the wrinkles with which I see myself. Like my father, he too is responsible for my eternal youth. He is kind in his feelings. He has never celebrated my birthday boisterously, so I have been able to forget to keep track of the years. He thinks I don't notice. But the truth is that at the end of the day I no longer know how old I am.

And he also avoids talking about my body, which has widened with the years. I don't wear the same styles as before. I have the dresses stored in the wardrobe, to be appreciated discreetly. Daily at seven o'clock in the evening he opens the door, knowing that I'm waiting for him on the other side. And when the television shows some bodies in full bloom, he buries his face in the newspaper, only we exist in the world.

I am grateful for the effort he makes in loving me. I struggle to thank him, though at times without wanting to, otherwise some strange face which isn't his, but that of an unknown man whose image I never want to see again, upsets me. Then I feel my mouth dry, dry from an everyday life that confirms the taste of the bread eaten the night before, which will nourish me tomorrow as well. A bread that he and I have eaten for so many years without complaint, annointed by love, bound by the wedding ceremony that declared us husband and wife. Ah, yes, I love my husband.

Translated by Claudia Van der Heuvel

The Message

Elena Poniatowska

I came to see you, Martin, and you are not here. I am sitting on the front step of your house, leaning against your door, and I think that in some place in the city, as if by a sound wave that passes through the air, you should know that I am here. This is your little garden; the mimosa is stretching and children passing by pull its closest branches. I see scattered around on the ground around the wall some very straight and formal flowers that have leaves like swords. They are navy blue and look like soldiers. They are very important, very honest. You are also a soldier. You are marching for your life one, two; one, two... Your whole garden is solid; it is like you with a strength that inspires confidence.

Here I am against the wall of your house, the way I sometimes lean against your back. The sun also strikes the windowpanes and because it is already late, it is gradually fading. The red-hot sun has warmed your honeysuckle, and its fragrance becomes even more penetrating. It is twilight. The day is drawing to a close. Your neighbor passes by. I don't know if she sees me. She is going to water her little garden. I remember that she brings you noodle soup when you are sick, and that her daughter gives you injections... I think about you very deliberately, as if I drew you inside of me and you remained drawn there. I would like to be sure that I am going to see you tomorrow, and the day after tomorrow and always in an uninterrupted chain of days; that I will be able to look at you slowly, even though I know every little corner of your face; that nothing between us has been provisional or accidental.

I am leaning over a piece of paper, and I am writing all this to you, and I think that now, in some city block where you may be walking in a hurry in your usual decisive way you are on one of those streets where I always imagine you to be: on the corner of Donceles and Cinco de Febrero or Venusiano Carranza Street, seated on any one of those monotonous gray benches which are broken only by the crowd of people hurrying to take the bus; you must know within yourself that I am waiting for you.

I came only to tell you that I love you, and because you are not here, I am writing to you. I can hardly write now because the sun already set. I'm not sure what I'm putting down. Outside more children come running by. And an iritated woman carrying a pot warns, "Don't shake my hand because I will spill the milk..." And I drop this pencil, Martin, and I drop the lined paper, and I let my arms hang uselessly along my body, and I'm waiting for you.

I'm thinking that I would love to hug you. Sometimes I would like to be older because youth carries within itself the imperious, implacable need to relate everything to love.

A dog barks; a hostile bark. I think that it's time for me to go. In a little while the neighbor will come to put on the lights of your house; she has the key and will put on the light in your bedroom, which faces out on the street, because in this neighborhood there are a lot of assaults and robberies. They rob the poor often; the poor rob each other... You know, since I was a child I have sat down like this to wait; I was always docile because I was waiting for you. I was waiting for you. I know that all women wait. They wait for future life, for all those images forged in solitude, for all that forest that moves toward them; for all that immense promise that is a man; a pomegranate that suddenly is opened and shows its shining red seeds; a pomegranate like a ripe mouth with a thousand sections. Later those hours lived through imagination, made into real hours, will have to take on weight and size and rawness. Oh, my love, we are so full of interior portraits, so full of unlived landscapes.

It is now nighttime, and I almost cannot see what I am scribbling on the lined paper. I cannot perceive the letters. There, where you may not understand, put in the white empty spaces: "I love you. . ." I don't know if I am going to slip this paper under your door; I don't know. You have made me respect you. . . Perhaps now that I am leaving, I may stop only to ask your neighbor to give you the message; that she tell you that I came.

Translated by Joy Renjilian-Burgy

The Key

Lygia Fagundes Telles

It was now too late to say that he was not going...it was now much too late. By allowing plans to go forward they had gone too far. And so what could he do about it at this late hour? Now he would be obliged to exchange the comfort of his pajamas for a tight collar and the warmth of the blankets for the chilly night. Oh, how chilly the nights had become recently. Tropical country indeed...where was it supposed to be tropical?—"The good weather has gone," he growled in the middle of a yawn. There had to be a social circle in hell, apparently the most bearable of all circles, but only apparently! Men and women dressed to kill; coming and going, chatting, circulating, chatting incessantly, exhausted yet unable to sit down or rest, drunk from drowsiness yet unable to fall asleep, their eyes and mouths wide-open, smiling...smiling...smiling... The circle of the fatuous and simple-minded, clothed in ties and laced shoes and condemned to tolerate and exchange nonsensical small-talk for ever more. "Amen," he whispered distractedly. He closed his eyes and pursed his lips. "But why do we have to go to this damn party? Can't you see that I'm exhausted?

Exhausted!" He wanted to cry out as he beat his clenched fists on the cushion of the armchair. He directed his pleading eyes to the woman in the room—"So you don't understand—exhausted."

"Tom! How about you starting to get dressed?" Of course she didn't understand a thing, cretin that she was. Party after party after party! All day long and all night long, it was nothing but one damn party after another—getting all dressed up, then undressed, only to start getting dressed up again, "Hurry Tom, we're late!" Late...! To have to shave, to choose a tie, and to pull in and strap up his poor paunch forcing it to escape into the first empty space available, that poor, miserable paunch which didn't even enjoy the right to slacken at its ease, not even that was allowed. Then the need to mime some cordial expression and to stand there smiling until five in the morning, his eyes wide open, those eyes of his which were lusterless from sheer exhaustion... And for what? "The bitches!" For they were nothing but a coterie of first-class bitches inventing dinner party after dinner party for the sake of sporting themselves in public.

"Dolled up like whores."

"What did you say, Tom?" the woman asked him coming back into the room. She was wearing only a flimsy black silk undergarment consisting of more lace than silk. "Have you started talking to yourself, eh?"

She gave him a sugary smile. But the moment she averted her gaze, his expression once more became gloomy. He threw his head back on the armchair and relaxed his muscles, yawning as he stretched out his legs. If only he might be allowed to sleep at least tonight, slip into bed with a hot-water bottle, a delightful hot-water bottle capable of creating that atmosphere of comforting warmth between his body and the blankets... The nicest thing in life was undoubtedly to be able to sleep, to sink like an anchor in the dark, to sink until one merged with darkness itself, and then to feel nothing more.

"I read in a magazine that women who don't get at least ten hours sleep at night, finish up with cellulitis before they're thirty."

Madge was brushing her hair. She paused, holding the brush

aloft, parted her thick mop of hair and peeped out. She drew a thread of hair from the brush and let it fall to the floor.

"Cellulitis."

"That's what I read!"

"Rubbish! In any case, that would never worry me, I have the firmest flesh imaginable, as you can see for yourself," she added, stretching out her bare leg in the direction of the armchair. "Just touch it and see... Some women have flesh softer than butter but mine is like mahogany, just test it for yourself!"

He stroked the shapely bronzed leg with his fingertips. He agreed with her, feigning astonishment, and then turned his uninterested gaze toward the window. The number of men who would give their all just to see those legs. Those famous legs! He lowered his eyes to examine his own feet and found himself on the point of smiling. In those socks they might well be the feet of some young blade, for Madge liked bright colors. Frances preferred discreet colors, but Madge was young and young women prefer gaudy colors, especially young women who live in the constant company of old men and are continually trying to disguise their partner's age by means of ingenuous artifices such as bright-colored socks, jazzy sports shirts, and loud ties. Brighten yourselves up old chaps! Brighten yourselves up! It won't be long now before she expects me to tint my hair.

"What's the dinner party for this time?"

"Well, I imagine that Renata wants to show off her new nose. Have you seen it yet?"

"Yes, I've seen it, and she looks frightful."

"Do you really think so?" said Madge, greatly surprised. She giggled. "The doctor cut off too much."

"I simply cannot understand why there should be so many dinner parties for no good reason."

"But does there have to be a special reason for giving a dinner party?" she said leaning forward. She began once more to brush her hair vigorously. "And after all, we are free this evening..."

Free are we? How cunningly Made expressed herself. Yet only a few years ago, how much tenderness had welled up inside him as he watched her biting her nails when he made her feel inhibited

...or biting her lower lip when she was stuck for an answer. And she was always stuck for an answer. She will blossom under my wing, he had thought, moved to the point of tears. She had blossomed without any doubt. He cast a glance in her direction. Yet he hadn't bargained for her blossoming to this extent.

With languid gesture, he buttoned the collar of his pajama jacket. He crouched his shoulders. How cold it had become.

She threw her hair back then proceeded to powder her feet with talcum. Then she began to rub the soles of her feet on the carpet with slow, sensual movements.

"Would you believe it, I don't even feel cold? Are we already into winter?"

"Bang in the middle of it."

"Well honestly, I don't feel the slightest bit cold."

"I believe you," he muttered, following her movements with his gaze. Bare-footed, semi-naked and radiant as if she were basking under the sun. She had so much energy, dear God...much too much energy, alas!...that exuberance which one associates with young animals possessing too much hair, too many teeth, too many gestures...too much of everything. They had only to breathe to be aggressive. Perhaps she might break a leg. But it was scarcely feasible for at that age, her bones must be made of iron. He yawned.

Madge was now rubbing cream on her face, and he watched her greasy fingers working in circular movements. Did she never feel the need to sleep? No, she didn't, in fact, and when she did sleep it was only to awaken impatiently, anxious to recover the hours lost in sleeping. A broken leg might offer a solution...

"Tom dear, you're dozing! Why don't you have a drink to liven you up a little."

He concealed his hands in the pockets of his pajamas. Making an effort, he opened his bleary eyes. "It's not a drink I need but some sleep!" he wanted to scream out, but instead of giving vent to his feelings, he smiled at her sweetly.

"No thanks Madge, I don't feel like drinking today."

"If you were to drink something I'm sure that you would feel much brighter."

"But I'm as bright as can be."

She dabbed toilet water on her hands and waved them around immediately so that they would dry. She knows that I'm watching her so she's deliberately showing off, he mused. She's nothing but an exhibitionist. If only she knew the date of her death—I'll bet she would rush out to donate her corpse to the School of Medicine in order to go on...

"I've splintered two nails," she complained, bending over to pull on her stockings. "And I simply cannot remember how it happened."

He closed his eyes. Frances' nails were short and obviously belonged to efficient hands, with their discreet film of clear nail polish. They were the nails and hands of an old woman. Frances had always possessed the hands of an old woman, and it was incredible how her hands had aged prematurely. Then her hair began to go gray. She could have done something about it. She did nothing whatsoever. She even seemed pleased to succumb to old age. That's what she had declared! I'm about to grow old. And she did. At that very moment, she must be playing a game of patience, her white hands shuffling the pack of cards. Chopin playing on the phonograph. It was comforting to fall asleep listening to Chopin, to sleep knowing that Frances was in the room, leaning over the cards while the piano poured forth that nostalgic cascade without further complications. Mozart created problems but Chopin was soothing, La—la...la...la—la—la—la—ra—ra...La—la—la—la—la...

"Tom, what do you think?"

He opened his eyes, startled.

"What?"

"My wig!" exclaimed Madge, arranging her hair with her hands. The long fringe threatened to fall into her swarthy eyes. "Do you like it?"

"Why do you need to wear a wig. Your own hair is so thick."

"Well it's fashionable. Besides with a wig I can easily vary the style."

He limply stretched out his arm to the bedside table. He grabbed the packet of cigarettes. It was empty. He closed it again. Just as well; he would smoke less. "At your age. . ." the doctor had started to say when he last consulted him.

"At your age. . ." It was useless trying to forget his age because everyone else around him did not appear to have forgotten. Ten years ago Madge's father had come up with the same remark although he hadn't had the courage to finish the sentence "At your age. . ." Madge was also in the room pretending to read one of those tawdry little magazines devoted to romance. "What's so wrong about being my age?" he had retorted provocatively. The old boy had clasped his knobbled hands over his belly. His fingernails were black. "The point is that my daughter is only eighteen years of age and you are forty nine. There is a considerable difference in your ages," he had pondered, scratching his head with his fingers outstretched like claws, just as a monkey would scratch itself. "For the moment it may not seem important, but how will it affect you both in ten years from now?" At that point Tom had grabbed his hat and coat, opened the door and with a dramatic gesture rejoined:

"In ten years time, the danger of my becoming a cuckold will be entirely my affair."

He stiffened in his chair. In ten years time was here and now.

"Do you think Ferdinand will be there too?"

"Freddy? I haven't the slightest idea. Why do you ask?" So the scoundrel already had a nickname. Freddy.

"Why Freddy? What's this?"

"But everyone calls him Freddy."

Everyone was Madge. She loved giving people nicknames and was never slow in coming out with intimate endearments.

"I simply cannot understand how a good-for-nothing like him has so much success with women. He's illiterate and nothing but a gigolo."

"A gigolo?"

"That's what they say."

"Oh really Tom, I find that difficult to believe."

"Well if he isn't a gigolo he sure looks like one. An out-and-out scoundrel twanging out blu—blu—blu on that guitar of his."

Pensively, she put on her shoes.

"He has a pleasant voice."

"What's pleasant about that voice? He has the voice of a pip-squeak, and one has to stand right beside him to hear anything. It's effeminate..."

Affeminate or effeminate? He yawned.

"When all is said and done, he's a perfect jackass. It makes me sick to see all those ridiculous females drooling over him in admiration. He has youth and nothing else. YOUTH..." he mumbled turning his lifeless gaze toward the mirror.

Madge adored mirrors, and there was a surfeit of them throughout the house. The one beside him was the worst of all, reflecting as it did one's entire image without missing a single detail. With that mirror Tom had learned that to grow old is to become out of focus: one's features become blurred and the outline of one's face finishes up by losing its shape like a ball of dough soaked in water.

"But Tom, are you never going to get dressed? It's almost nine o'clock."

"I shall be ready in a second...the time you take to make up your face gives me plenty of time."

"And what about that beard? Aren't you going to shave?"

"Is it really necessary?" he groaned, passing his hand over his chin. "I've already shaved once today, and my skin is becoming all marked from so much shaving."

"So you really mean to go out looking like some ruffian off the street. You look like an old man."

"I am an old man."

"Oh, my precious one, you mustn't say that. Come along now, get up and go and have your little shave," she pleaded with him caressing him on the head.

"No!"

"Really I've never known anyone to be so stubborn."

"What are we going to do at this dinner, just tell me that?"

"To eat and then..."

"But you know damn well that I cannot eat anything while I'm on a diet. What I need is some sleep, can't you understand?"

"Well, sleep then!"

He looked into her face. She was smiling. That was exactly what she wanted.

"I'm still going to be ready before you," he threatened her, resting his hands on the armchair. He started to get up. . .only to fall back into the chair once more. He closed his eyes and yawned. He would count up to five and then rise like a thunderbolt. Well perhaps up to ten. He rubbed his eyes.

"Good heavens!"

"Are you in pain, Tom?"

He cast her a long appraising glance.

"You look lovely."

"Me, lovely?"

She was still smiling. Women always refused to take part in the game. Frances was just the opposite of Madge, yet she too, had worn the same expression the last time that he had said to her "Frances my darling, you are lovely." Those words had caused her to lower her head to one side with a bit of irritation: "Oh, Thomas, me? Lovely?. . ." He prevented her from protesting further: "Yes lovely. When you take a little trouble with your appearance you can look lovely, and you ought to dress up more often, my sweet. Look at all the other women around you!"

Frances had put her glasses back on again. "At my age Thomas?"

That obsession of hers with age. Why did she have to keep on referring to her age? At times it became irritating.

"After all darling, remember that I too am nearing my fiftieth birthday. Would you like me to cover my head in ashes and sit at home waiting for death?" She had put a record on the phonograph. "Thomas have you noticed what a lovely night it is? Why don't you take a walk round the block." He went. During his walk he met Madge. He experienced the sensation of being reborn when she called him Tom. He suddenly felt himself to be a new man. A New Man! Which advertisement carried that phrase? I Became A New Man! He had seen the advertisement on a train. It obviously referred to some medicine or other. . . It was such a long time ago. The urge to travel on a train and while away the time reading the advertisements and those notices expressing so much consideration and prudence.—Please Wait Until The Train Has Come To A Complete Halt. A time of prudence and consideration. There was a nice feeling as one went gliding through the deserted streets, swaying from left to right as if in a cradle...

"Now Tom, make up your mind at once because Renata gets furious when her guests arrive late."

"To hell with Renata!"

"Tom!"

"To hell with Renata and all her lousy guests!"

"Really, how disagreeable you're being," the youthful Madge exclaimed, throwing the powder dish on the bed. She zipped her dress, "You simply have no idea how disagreeable you have become recently."

"I'm tired," he wanted to say. Shivering, he pulled the collar of his pajama jacket up over his ears. He opened his mouth to yawn, his hands cupped over his mouth, warming them with his breath. He would sleep the whole night through, and the following night and the one after that... He would sleep night after night until he died of sleep. Chopin playing on the phonograph and Frances at his side, enjoying her game of patience. How he adored that pleasant sound of the cards rustling on the table while Frances murmured things which demanded no reply. She was waiting for a jack and got a queen instead: "I didn't need you," she scolded. The old-fashioned furniture, Frances' unfashionable clothes. Her frumpish appearance. "But Frances dear, you ought to wear something more up-to-date and use more cosmetics!" He bought her a flask of potent perfume... He bought her a lipstick which he had seen advertised in a magazine, in a new shade—Which Makes Even The Statues Sit Up And Take Notice—to quote the advertisement. He gave her a coral necklace made of interwoven strands of innumerable coral beads. "We are still in our prime my darling! We must fight the onslaught of old age." She looked at him with a reticent expression. Or was it irony? No, probably not even that, for Frances was much too generous by nature to be ironic. She looked at him almost like a mother contemplating her own child before handing him the key to the front door.

"Tom, do you think these gloves match my outfit?... Tom, I am speaking to you, answer me!"

"They match, my love, they make a perfect match."

"Perhaps I should wear the green ones..."

"Those are an excellent match."

Almost like a mother contemplating her own child. Then he lowered his head and went out. On the street, he felt like an adolescent clutching the key in his pocket. "I'm free," he felt like shouting to the passers-by, to the passing cars, to the passing wind. "Free, free!"

Oh, if only he could return to her without either words or explanation. She too, would say nothing: as if he had only gone out to buy a packet of cigarettes.

"Is everything alright, Frances dear?" he would enquire upon seeing her frown slightly. She would peer closely at her cards: "I only need one card to finish..."

Madge's voice, on the other hand, struck him as being anonymous. Unreal. He heard his own voice, husky but tranquil, say to her "You go, darling and enjoy yourself."

She still insisted. Had she really insisted? The heels of her shoes echoed in the silence like the sound of muffled tapping as they quickly escaped. He stretched out his hand to the bed and tugged at the cover. He pulled it over himself. Everything was dark and still, as if in the depths of the ocean. The perfume in the air softened and there hovered the perfume of a garden of statues, resplendent white statues who slept with vacant eyes and no pretext would succeed in making them open their eyes. Tom lazily stretched his legs. Madge's legs resuscitated in the darkness: she danced naked, rubbing her feet on the carpet while the guitar music insinuated up her legs like stockings. Tom suddenly became agitated and tried to shut the door in the face of the man with black fingernails "That's my problem!" The discordant music was already halfway up the legs of the columns:

"Be careful, Madge! Not Ferdinand whatever you do!..." The dancer and music settled like dust on the antique table. The pack of cards opened, rustling like a fan. And kings with woolen feet emerged from the card pack dragging their ermine cloaks. Tom wrapped himself up in one of their cloaks and stood smiling at Frances. She was smiling too, in her dress of rose-coloured muslin and lightly nibbling the corner of a card. "May I?" he asked, resting his head on her lap...

As he handed her back the key.

Translated by Giovanni Pontiero

Solitude of Blood

Marta Brunet

The base was made of bronze, with a drawing of lacework flowers. The same flowers were painted on the reservoir glass, and a white spherical shade interrupted its extremities to allow the chimney to pass through. That lamp was the showpiece of the house. Placed in the center of the table, on top of a meticulously elaborate crocheted table cover, it was turned on only when there was a dinner guest, an unexpected, remote occurrence. But it was also lighted on Saturday night, every Saturday, because that eve of a worry-free morning could be celebrated in some way, and nothing could be better then, than to have the lamp spreading its brightness over the vivid tangle of paper that covered the walls, over the china cabinet so symmetrically decorated with fruit plates, soup tureens and formal stacks of dishes; over the doors of the cupboard, with decorative panels and the iron latch and its lock speaking of the same times as the grating that protected the window on the garden side of the house. Yes, every Saturday night, the lamplight traced out for the man and the woman a little hollow of intimacy, generally peaceful.

From living in contact with the earth, the man seemed made of telluric elements. In the south, in the mountains, looking at their reflection in the translucent eye of the lakes, the trees, polished by wind and by water, had strange shapes and startling qualities. In that wood worked by the pitiless harsh weather the man was carved. The years had made furrows in his face, and from that fallow field sprouted his beard, moustache, eyebrows, eyelashes. And his tangled mat of hair, coal black, crowned his head with a rebellious shock, which was always escaping over his forehead and which he would push back into place with a characteristic mechanical gesture.

Now, in the brightness of the lamplight, the large hands carefully shuffled a deck of cards. He spread the cards out over the table. Absorbed in the game of solitaire, slow and meticulous, because he was about to win, his features swelled with a kind of pleasantness. He hardly had any cards left in his hand. He drew one. He turned it over and suddenly the pleasantness turned into harshness. He gazed at the cards with rapt attention, the new card in his hand. He put down his remaining cards and tossed the big shock back, sinking and fixing his fingers in his hair. The pleasantness spread over his face again. He lifted his eyelids, and his eyes appeared like grapes, azure-blue. A cautious glance that became fixed on the woman, that found the woman's eyes, grey, so clear that in certain light or from a distance they gave the unsettling sensation of being blind.

"Just imagine that I'm not looking at you and go on with your trick...," said the woman with a voice that sang.

"Will it turn out really badly? asked the man.

"If it does, it does."

"It always fails to work for me! Come on, for God's sake! I'll do it again!" And he gathered the cards together to shuffle them.

Sometimes the game of solitaire "came out." Other times it "turned stubborn." But always at ten o'clock, the hours resonating in the corridor as they fell from the old clock, the man pulled himself up, looked at the woman, came toward her until he could put a hand on her head, and he caressed her hair, again and again, to conclude by saying, as he said that night:

"Until tomorrow, little one. Don't stay up for a long time, be sure the lamp is completely out and don't make a lot of noise with your phonograph. Let me drop off to sleep first..."

He left, closing the door. She heard his long strides through the corridor. Then she heard him go out onto the patio, saying something to the dog, turning around, going back and forth through the bedroom; she heard the bed creak, his heavy shoes falling one after the other, the bed creaking again, the man turning over, becoming quiet. The woman had abandoned the knitting in her lap. She was scarcely breathing, her mouth partially open, her whole self gathering in the sounds, separating them, classifying them, her auditory perception fine-tuned to such a point that all her senses seemed to have been transformed into one big ear. Tall, strong, her naturally brown skin tanned by the sun, she might have been any ordinary creole woman if her eyes had not set her apart, creating for her a face that memory, immediately, put in a place all by itself. Tension caused a little bead of perspiration to break out on her forehead. That was all. But she felt her chilled skin and, with an unconscious gesture, passed her hand slowly over it. Then, just as absent-mindedly, she looked at that hand. With every moment she seemed more tense, more like an antenna to receive signals. And the signal came. From the bedroom, and in the form of a snoring sound, which was followed, arrhythmically, by others.

Her muscles went limp. Her senses opened up into an exact five-pointed star, each one doing its particular job. But the woman still remained motionless, with her expanding pupils fixed on the lamp.

When had she bought that lamp? One time when she went to the town, when she sold her habitual dozen children's outfits, knitted between one household chore and another, between chores that were always the same, methodically distributed over days that were indistinguishable one from another. She bought that lamp as she had bought the china cabinet, and the wicker furniture, and the wardrobe with the mirror, and the quilted eiderdown comforter. Yes, as she had bought so many things, so much... Of course, over so many years! How many years had it been? Eighteen. She was thirty-six now, and she was eighteen when she got married. Eighteen and eighteen. Yes... The lamp. The china cabinet. The wicker furniture... She never believed, of this she was sure, that by knitting she could earn money not only to dress herself, but to give herself household conveniences.

He said, no sooner had they gotten married:

"You have to be enterprising in order to establish your own little business and earn money for your necessities. Raise chickens or sell eggs."

She answered:

"You know I'm ignorant about these things."

"Look for something that you know how to do then. Something they taught you in school."

"I could sell candy."

"Give up on selling in this god-forsaken place. It ought to be something that can be carried all together once a month to the town."

"I could knit."

"That's not a bad idea. But it's necessary to buy wool," he added, suddenly uneasy. "How much would you need to get started?"

"I don't know. Let me check prices. And ask around in the store, to see if people are interested in knitted articles."

"If it doesn't come out being really expensive..."

And it did not turn out to be expensive, and it was definitely a good business enterprise. The wife of the store owner himself bought the first completed item for her son, which was merely a sample. A lovely little suit, such as no child had ever had in that "god-forsaken place," where the people handled money and acquired tasteless things in shops in which the barrel of fat was next to the bottles of perfume and the cheap woolens were next to the medicinal balm. Her business was a big success. People placed orders with her. She knitted for the whole region. She was able to raise her prices. She never had enough supplies for the orders that were pending. When he saw that she was prospering, he said one day:

"It's a good idea for you to give me back the ten pesos I lent you to begin your knitting. And don't spend all the money that you earn just on things for yourself. Of course I'm not going to tell you to give me this money, it's yours, yes, you've well earned it, and I'm not going to tell you to hand it over to me." He always repeated what he had just expressed, insisting, wanting to impress the idea on his own mind. "But now you see, now it's necessary to buy a big kettle and to fix the cellar door. You could easily assume responsibility for the household affairs, now that you have so much money at your disposal. Yes. . . , so much money."

She bought the big kettle, she had the cellar door repaired. And then, she bought, and she bought. . . Because it represented happiness to her to be converting that mess of a country house, eaten up by neglect, into what it was now, a house like hers there in the north, in the little town shaded by willows and acacias, with the river singing or rumbling down the valley, and the Andes right there, ever present, background for the little houses that seemed like toys: blue pink, yellow, with wide entrance halls and a jasmine bush perfuming the siestas, and facing the patio gate, a painted green bench, inviting casual conversation in the early evening, when the birds and the angelus were taking flight through the skies in the same air, and the peaks took on violent pinks and gentle violet colors, before falling asleep beneath the blanket of watchful gleaming stars.

She closed her eyelids, as if she too should fall asleep in the shelter of that vigilance. But she opened them again right away and listened again, certain of hearing the rhythm of the one who was sleeping. Then she picked herself up and with silent movements opened the cupboard, and from the highest shelf she went about taking down and placing on the table an old phonograph, improbably shaped, like a little cabinet whose open main doors revealed a set of zither strings, at an oblique angle over the mouth of the receiver, which was nothing but a small open circle in the sound chamber. Below, other doors, smaller, afforded a view of the green turntable. That phonograph was her own luxury item, not like the lamp, luxury of the house, but hers, hers. Purchased when the señora from "los Tapiales," passing through the town, had found her in the store and seen her knitted articles and asked her if she could make some overcoats for her little girls. What a beautiful woman, with a mouth so large and tender and a voice that dragged out her "rr's," as if she were a French lady; but she wasn't, and that really made her laugh. What a workload she had that summer! That was when she saw fulfilled her longing to have a phonograph with records and everything. He permitted her to buy it. That was what she earned all that money for!

"Just buy it, my dear. What's yours is yours, of course, but it would be good if you could also see about buying a poncho for me, for the wool flannel one is wearing through. Because the poncho is a real necessity, and since I have to get together money for another pair of oxen, it's not a matter of squandering funds, and since you are earning so much... But it's clear, yes, that you'll buy yourself the phonograph too, and before anything else..."

First she bought the poncho and immediately afterwards the phonograph. Never greater was her pleasure than being back at home, the phonograph set up on the table, listening insatiably to the cadence of the waltz or the march that was abruptly interrupted to let the sound of tolling bells be heard. They had sold it to her with the right to two records that she might choose carefully; yet he was impatient on seeing her indecisive after choosing the first one—which was the one with waltz and the march on it—having to try out a whole album one record after another. Until he said, getting more and more impatient:

"It's getting late. Look how the sun is going down. We've got to go, yes. Night will catch us here if we don't. Take that one that you have set aside, and this one. One because you like it, and the other let's leave up to chance...," and he pulled out at random a record from the box.

Which turned out to have Spanish songs filled with laments, which neither he nor she liked and which she tried in vain to exchange. And when, some time later, she hinted timidly at the idea of buying more records, he—with the claylike expression that he was accustomed to wearing when he was being negative—answered severely:

"No more fuss in the house. What you've got is enough and

with that you can get along."

She never insisted. When she was alone, when he and his laborers were in the field working, she would take out the phonograph and in a standing position, with a vague uneasiness that she was "wasting time"—as he said—her hands together and a spiral of joy beginning to stir in her breast, she let herself sink sweetly into the music.

He did not like at all this "wasting time." She knew this well and did not allow herself to be carried away by the overwhelming desire to hear the waltz or to hear the march. But out of that habit of telling him, in minute detail, whatever she had done during the day, a habit to which he had made her accustomed since the beginning of their married life, she said, her eyelids open and her pupils dilated:

"I ground the flour for the workers, I mended your coat, I kneaded dough for the house..." She paused imperceptibly and added very gently: "I listened to the phonograph for a while and that's all..."

"Wanting to waste time..., time that's useful for so many things that bring in money, yes, to waste it..." He said it in different tones of voice, sometimes ascertaining a weakness in the woman, gently protective and condescending; sometimes absent-minded, mechanical, tossing back the rebellious shock of hair, troubled by another idea; sometimes stern, wooden and frightening her, she who had never been able to prevail over a dark, instinctive submissiveness of female animal to male, who in former years humiliated herself to her father and in the present, to her husband.

When she, without any hinting, bought that leather jacket for him, shiny as if it were waxed, black and long, which the storekeeper said was for a mechanic and which the rain could not seep into, like that which might fall in the stubborn downpours of the region; when she bought it and mysteriously brought it home and left the package in front of his place at the table—so that he might find it by surprise—the man, his mood softening on seeing it, passed his big hand over her soft hair, done up in braids and raised like a tiara on her head.

"You're a good old gal. Hard-working, like women ought to be, yes. And listen, little one, tonight since its Saturday, light the lamp, and that way I can do my solitaire better. And when I go off to bed, you'll stay for a little while longer and play your phonograph. Yes, you'll play it, but when I'm sound asleep. You should have your pleasure too..."

Thus the custom was born.

She lowered the lamp's light a little. She went on tiptoes to the window and opened it, letting in the night and its silence. She went back to the table, carefully wound up the phonograph, put her hands together and waited.

Ta-ta..., ta-ta..., ta-ta-dum...

The march. And suddenly everything around her was blotted out; it disappeared submerged in the stridency of the trumpets and the roll of the drums, dragging her back through time, until leaving her in the plaza of the northern town, after eleven o'clock mass on a rainless Sunday, the drum major spinning the baton around and following after him, marching in step, the band taking the final turn along the parade route, with the children swarming in front, and a dog mixed in among their racing feet, while the ladies on their traditional bench commented on petty problems, the gentlemen talked about the wine harvest, and they—she and her sisters, she and her friends, arm in arm, with their braids uneasily sliding over breasts that were already swelling with sighs—passed and passed again in front of the grown-ups, crossing through groups of boys, who seemed not to see them, and on fixing their gaze on their surroundings only looked at one of them, absorbing them as if thirsty for fresh water, from a real spring, mouths avid, grown large with desire.

It was the occasion when new clothes were shown off. Sometimes they were pink or celestial blue. Sometimes they were red or sea colored, and this meant that throughout a sky of faded blue a few clouds shed their fleece and that the wind had carried away the last leaf of dark gold. She particularly remembered a red overcoat, with a round collar of white fur, curly and soft against her face and a muff like a little barrel, hanging from the collar by a cord, also white. And the warning from the mother:

"Put your hands in the muff and don't you take them out again.

Of course, you can say hello to people. . .," she added after a thoughtful pause.

They went back and forth, arm in arm. They whispered incomprehensible things, inaudible confidences that drew their heads together, murmurs scarcely articulated and that suddenly shook them in long bursts of laughter that left the trees perplexed, because it wasn't nesting season, or they stirred the trees to nod approvingly during that other time of year when the birds tried to add their own comments to those musical sounds. Sometimes, no, once, she raised her face to better catch the laughter that always seemed to fall on her from above, and from this foreshortened perspective, her pupils found the gaze of a pair of green eyes, as green as new grass and in the face of a boy darkened by the sun, strong and like a freshly sprouting field. Only an instant. But an instant to be carried home and treasured and placed in the depths of her heart, and to feel that a pang of anguish and a feeling of warmth and a vague desire to cry and pass soft fingertips over her lips suddenly tormented her, in the middle of reading, a chore, or a dream. To see him again. To have the feeling impressed on her again that life was stopping in her veins. For that second in which the green gaze of the boy fixed on her was the reason for her existence. Who was he? Was he from the town? No. Someone familiar? No. Perhaps a summer vacationer from a nearby area. She guarded her secret treasure. She talked less, she rarely laughed. But her pupils seemed to become enlarged, to flood her face in that search for the vigorous silhouette, dressed as the boys from the town did not dress. He arrived in a tiny car. It left him beside the club. He went to mass. She observed him from a distance, attentive and circumspect, in the presbytery, a little on the fringe of the group of men. When mass was over, he went to the candy store, filled the car up with packages, then took a walk around the plaza in order to go to the post office, retraced his steps, got into the car and left.

It was obvious that the other girls had noticed him. And dying of laughter over what he was wearing, in his golf or riding pants, they called him "Baggy Pants." To her hidden desperation.

The march continued filling the house with harmonious sounds.

The bells burst in. As if pealing. Like on certain Sundays, when there was High Mass; but these were more sonorous bells, more harmonious, as if while they were pealing, pulsations of untapped joy were mixed with them.

The march ended. She shifted the needle, wound it again, turned the record over, and now the waltz began to spin around the table, music that seemed to be dancing, a beat that created soap bubbles, sometimes slowly, sometimes rapidly, radiating their colors.

She never found out what his name was, who he was, where he was from. One Sunday he didn't appear. Or the next. Or any other. A young girl raised the point:

"I wonder what's become of 'Baggy Pants'?"

"La Calchona, the Witch, has probably eaten him up," answered another, and they burst out laughing.

Her chest ached, and the sharp claw of sorrow dug at her throat. The corners of her mouth drew taut, and her eyes, like never before, filled her face. Once in the house, she sought out the most secluded corner, in the storage room, between the piano box and a pile of mattresses, and there she released her sorrow, she opened her heart, allowing her pain to escape and envelop her in its viscous mantle, adhering to her like new skin, moist and painful. The tears rained down her face. Never to see him again. The sobbing became stronger. What gaze was going to hold that magic for her? That burning that raged within her, she did not know where, as if waiting longingly for some unknown happiness. His name?... Enrique... Juan... José... Humberto... And if his name was Romauldo, like her grandfather's? It did not matter. She would always love him, whatever his name was... She would love him... Love him... Love him the way a woman loves, because she already was a woman and her fifteen years were ripening in her budding breasts, bringing a downy softness to her intimate zones and giving her voice a sudden dark tremolo. She would love him forever. She seemed to disintegrate into weeping. And suddenly she became still, sighing and still, without tears, her sorrow diluted, formless and distant. She sighed again. She wiped her eyes. And she found herself thinking that probably they were looking for her all over the house, that she ought to go wash her tear-scorched face, that . . . Yes, it was shameful to confess it, but she was hungry. And she went out gently from among the stored items, watching carefully in order to leave without being seen and to go refresh her face in the courtyard water tank. Her mother stared at her occasionally, seeming confused, and would murmur repeatedly:

"What a woman my little girl's become . . ."

The father was more definitive in his conclusion and said at the top of his voice:

"Look, Maclovia, we have to marry this one off as soon as possible."

For years she wept her sorrow between the piano box and the stack of mattresses. Nobody ever found out anything. They lifted up her braids, which since then she wore like a tiara around her head. They lowered the hems of all her dresses. No one said that she was pretty. But there wasn't a man who did not become startled on seeing her, lost in the contemplation of her grey eyes, experiencing something akin to vertigo in the presence of her mouth, fleshy, intensely red. Her appearance was courteous and indifferent. She had to protect her memory, to keep her dream-fantasy safe, and only in a land of silence could she do this. Men looked at her, they stopped right next to her, but all of them, unanimously, went after other girls who were more accessible to their courtship.

The father introduced the future husband one day. He was from lands to the south, proprietor of a ranch, part of the estate of an old family in the region. Already an older man, of course not a "veteran"; this is what her mother said. As she also added: "A good catch."

Indifferent, she allowed them to interpret her acquiescence among themselves and they married her off. This man or another, it made no difference to her. For not a one of them was hers, the one she loved, that green gaze that filled her blood with tenderness. This one? The other one? What did it matter? And she had to get married, according to what her mother said, smiling and persuasive, and according to what her father ordered with his thundering voice that did not accept dissenting opinions.

She remembered the discomfort of her bridal gown, the crown that pressed against her temples and her terrible fear of ripping the veil. The groom whispered:

"It was so expensive..., be careful with it..."

The waltz ended. For a moment silence filled the house, a silence so complete that it was injurious. Because it was so complete that the woman began to sense the presence of her heart, and terror forced open her mouth, and then she heard the panting sound of her breathing. But she also perceived the snoring in the other room, broken off when the music was interrupted and which a soothed subconscious mind imposed again upon the sleeping man. Then she heard a cricket in the courtyard. She raised herself up slowly and looked, outside, at the black and spacious field that she knew was flat, without anything in the distance but the ring of the horizon. Flat. A plain. And in the midst of it herself and her vigil, intercepting memories, caressing the past. Lost on the plain. With no one for her tenderness, to look at her and kindle within her that passion that had moved through her blood before and made her mouth shudder under the trembling touch of her fingers. Alone.

She went back to the phonograph. She would have liked to repeat the magical experience. To spread out again the melodic canvas in order to project the images there once more. But no. The clock struck once. Ten thirty. If he were to wake up...

With the same caution as someone who handles living, fragile creatures, she put away the phonograph and the records, she closed the cupboard, and she put the key in her pocket. From the china cabinet she took out a small candle stick and lit the candle.

Then she turned off the lamp.

And she went out to the corridor, following after the light's mysterious glow, pursued by nightmarish shadows impinging on one another.

*   *   *

When she carried the rice pudding to the dining room, she

believed she had made the last trip of the evening and that then she could sit down to wait for the guest to leave. But the two men, the lamp between them, dug in their spoons happily, like children, and once they had cleaned their plates, they both raised their heads and sat staring at her, eagerly, their mouths watering.

"Serve yourselves a little more," she said, bringing the platter up beside them.

"Of course, patrona; it's really a pleasure to eat this!' admitted the guest.

"It's that the old gal has a good hand for these things!" And the man added in a confidential manner, because the wine was spreading through his body: "Things that they taught her in school; its worth the trouble to have an educated wife, friend; yes, I'm telling you, and believe me."

She waited, uncomfortable in her chair, her hands placed politely on the tablecloth. During the day they had eaten abundantly from a side of beef and the wine in the big jug was almost gone. It would be a matter of waiting around for awhile for the obligatory after dinner conversation and then the guest would leave. For his house was far away and the night was becoming windy, and over a background of pale stars enormous threatening clouds were creating shapes and then destroying them.

The man's voice caught her attention:

"And that coffee? Hurry, for the train won't wait..." And he laughed at his statement, hitting the table with his fist and making the lamp wobble back and forth.

Her trips to the kitchen weren't over.... She went out to the corridor, thinking, disheartened, that the fire was probably already out and to revive it was a task that would take awhile. But under the ashes the red throbbing of the embers made her almost smile, and the water promptly boiled, and the coffee pot, important-looking with its two tiers, was on the tray, and she was once again walking through the darkened house, for the light of the reflector only seemed to thicken the blackness in the corners.

In the dining room the two men deliberated, sparing their words, their creole sullenness still in effect, because that meal was designated to close a deal for the purchase of some pigs that the guest had come from the town to see, and the afternoon had been spent in calculations, "I'll ask for this and offer you that," and they still were not arriving at anything concrete.

"On Monday I'll send you a messenger with the answer," said the guest.

"It's that tomorrow, Sunday, I have to give an answer to one of the parties that's also interested, and I can't put it off any longer, you understand, certainly; it's not good to just leave him waiting and to have him back out and you too and I lose a good buyer. . ."

"It's that you insist on such prices. . ."

"What the pigs are worth, friend; you won't find any better ones. There's not another litter like this anywhere around here, as you well know, yes. . ."

The woman had brought out the cups, the sugar; now she served them the coffee. Let them settle their business quickly and have the guest be on his way! And she sat down again, in the same position as before, so identical to, so like a cardboard cut-out and placed there, so erect, inexpressive and mysterious that, suddenly, the two men turned around to look at her, as if attracted by the ecstatic force that emanated from her.

The guest said:

"The patrona is so quiet!"

And the man, vaguely uncomfortable without knowing why:

"Serve some aguardiente, then."

She got up again, but this time not to go to the kitchen. She opened the cupboard and stood on her tiptoes to reach up above her the bottle that was stuck away in a corner behind the phonograph. The guest, who was watching her do it, asked solicitously:

"Do you want me to help you, patrona? The bottle is pretty high up for you."

"Look at it, how troublesome the bottle is. . ., just like a woman. But that's what I'm here for, yes. . .," exclaimed the man, and he reached up to take it down.

His hands bumped into the phonograph, and he added, delighted to find another token of respect to offer the guest:

"Let's tell the patrona to play the phonograph for us a little. I call it 'her noisemaker,' because you've got to see how it squawks; but she likes it and I let her get her pleasure out of it. That's the way I am, yes. Play something for my friend to hear. Put on what's prettiest. But first you'll serve us something, yes..."

He placed the bottle and the phonograph on the edge of the table. The woman had remained quiet, listening to what the man was saying. But when the big hands seized the little cabinet, a kind of resentment began to stir in her breast, slowly, hardly at all at first. The phonograph was her own property and nobody had any right to it. Never had anyone operated it, except for herself with her own hands, which were loving, as if for touching a child. She swallowed hard and then clenched her teeth, revealing the hard edge of her jaw, just like her father's and just like that of the distant grandfather who had come from the Basque Country. She thought that the aguardiente would make them forget the music and instead of the little glasses, green and deceiving, into which a thimbleful of liquid hardly fit, she set out the other big wineglasses and filled them halfway. The men sniffed the aguardiente, then raised their eyes at the same time as they clinked the glasses, and in unison said:

"To your health!"

And they emptied their contents in one gulp.

"This is aguardiente!" the man said.

The guest answered with a whistle that seemed to get stuck in his puckered mouth, a gesture of stupor, because something was beginning to dance in his muscles without any intervention of his will, and this left him in this state, perplexed and so happy on the inside.

"Let's talk about the deal again," the man proposed. "It's a good idea now to get it decided, yes; my price is reasonable, as you well know and you know you're getting pigs that'll bring double the price, yes; fattened up in the feed pen and the boar almost a purebred, outstanding pigs for ham..."

The other man smiled leisurely and nodded his assent.

"It's a deal, then?" asked the man. "It's a deal?"

"The aguardiente's good; one doesn't drink any better around here, not even in the Piñeiros' hotel."

It was strange what he was feeling: still that sort of muscular movement that now was polarizing in his knees and was hurling his legs in every direction, irreducibly, just like a clown. And he was so happy!

"Good aguardiente, of course, yes...; it's a gift from my father-in-law, who's from the vineyard region and he trades in wines. Of the best quality. The deal is set?"

"What deal?" he asked stupidly, attentive to his desire to laugh, to the impossibility of his laughing and to the disconsolate feeling that was beginning to inundate him. And his legs under the table dancing, dancing...

"The deal about the pigs, yes..."

"Oh! Really... But wasn't the patrona going to play the..., how did you call it..., the..., well... the phonograph?"

The woman hated him with a violence that might have destroyed him on becoming tangible. All the bad words that she had heard in her existence, and that she never said, suddenly came to her memory and they felt so alive to her that she was astonished they did not turn around to look at her, terrified and speechless in the face of this rude avalanche.

"It's a deal?"

"Music..., music..., life is short and one must enjoy it..."

But instead of reaching her hand out to the phonograph, the woman had extended it toward the bottle and again she served them, causing the wine glasses to overflow. And since each one, absorbed in his own thoughts, had not seen that the glass had been set in front of him, it was she who said, suddenly cordial:

"Serve yourselves!" And she made an inconclusive gesture of invitation, a kind of greeting that stayed in the air, paralyzed, while she watched them drink: "To your health!" And the hoarse sound of her voice saying the toast surprised her.

"It's a deal?" insisted the man, his tongue tangled in his consonants.

The other man did not hear a thing but only felt the tide of distress growing, at the same time as in his ears a cicada began its steady mid-afternoon sawing. And why were his legs dancing?

"Brother, I'm a good man... I don't deserve this..." And the distress spilled over into a hiccough. I don't want my legs to dance, my legs are mine, mine... Music...," he shouted suddenly and he got up halfway, but he lost his momentum and fell down on top of the table.

The woman watched them, silent, with her eyes so open and inexpressive, so bright, so enormous in their greyness. They were not to come near her phonograph again, they were not to have it; it was hers; therein resided her inner life, her deliverance from colorless days. Outwardly she was similar to the plain, flat, with her husband's will cutting her level like the wind; but just as the current of water in all its forms passes under the layers of the earth, so she had within herself her singing water saying things from the past. The music belonged to her. To her, and pity anyone who came near it!

But the guest extended a heavy hand and placed it on the little doors of the phonograph, trying to open them. But he did not open them, because she, standing up violently and grabbing his hand harshly, said—also harshly:

"No. It's mine."

The guest looked at her, with his mouth curled up and trying to think some thought that he had just forgotten. Suddenly he remembered. And again he stretched out the hand that she had removed from the little door latch.

"I'm telling you, no!"

"Look how she's insulting me, brother..."

The man insisted greedily:

"It's a deal?"

"Music...," answered the guest, stubbornly.

"Why don't you play something? Go ahead and raise a ruckus, little one, yes; something you like. Don't you see that we're going to close the deal?"

He would not put his hands on the phonograph. Not that, never. The guest had picked himself up and this time his muscles did obey him. But the woman prevented the attack and put herself in-between, defensively. The other man reeled about the dining room, until bumping into the wall, and he turned around, inflamed with a criminal impulse, blinded to everything that was not his own idea.

"Music..., music.."

"Has she gone crazy? What's happening to her?" asked the man.

The guest was on top of her and she on top of the phonograph, defending it with her whole body. They struggled. The man looked at them for an instant, stunned, repeating:

"Has she gone crazy? Has she gone crazy?"

But when the guest gave a sharp cry because the woman's teeth were ripping into his hand, he rushed forward to separate them, to defend his friend, to defend his transaction, his deal already almost completed.

She kicked and bit them, behaving like an animal, furious, they way a puma in the wild might defend her cubs. The men did not know why they were getting punched, why they were rolling on the floor, why the table was reeling and the lamp was shifting its light back and forth in a swaying movement that was worse than the sensation in their stomachs. The phonograph fell with a crash and the strings reverberated, like the lament of a grove of trees whose leaves are ripped off by a strong wind. The guest was sitting on the floor, bewildered, and suddenly his cry broke into sobs that interrupted his hiccoughs. The man leaned against the window, astonished by everything and looking at the woman, her clothing in shreds, the magnificence of her hairdo undone, with a long slash on her face, cleaning herself off with the apron that was red with blood, her blouse stained, stubbornly intent on gathering from the floor the pieces of the broken records, looking at them and sobbing, cleaning the blood off herself, sobbing and looking for more pieces and cleaning off the blood and sobbing.

But the guest diverted his attention with his enormous hiccoughs.

"Brother..., I thought I was in the home of a brother... I've been insulted... I have...," he lamented, stumbling as he spoke.

"Don't cry anymore, brother." And suddenly back to his idea

and full of solicitude and tenderness: "It's a deal?"

"Swine, that's just what you are: swine...," shouted the woman, and with her armload of pieces she left the dining room, closing the door with a resounding bang that startled the rats in the loft and caused the dog to gaze at her steadily, its sequin eyes sparkling in the gloom.

* * *

Outside the wind's mane was whipping about, unleashed in a frenetic gallop. The clouds had pressed themselves tightly together, dense and black, imparting a dark tint to the environs and not allowing the outline of a single thing to be seen. As if the elements had not yet been set apart. A cricket was giving witness, immutably, to its existence.

She fled, pressing the shattered records against her chest as she went, feeling the flow of the blood through the wound, warm and sticky on her neck, making its way inside to the fine skin of her chest. She walked with her head down, breaking through the blackness and the wind. She walked. The house was far away, not just erased by the darkness. The cricket, imperceptible, was left behind tenaciously useless. She could be out on the plain and be the living center of her desolate surroundings; she could be in a valley bounded by rivers and precipices; she could walk, walk, endlessly, until she fell exhausted upon the hard earth, being grown over evenly with identical weeds; she could suddenly slide down the slope of the ravine and go crashing onto the smooth stones of a river engorged with reddish sand; she could... Anything could happen in this blackness of chaos, confusing and dreadful. For to her nothing mattered.

To end it all. To die against the earth. To be destroyed in the ravine. Not to feel any more that corrosive ardor, bitter to her mouth and clawing around inside her. To end it all. Not to make an effort any more to know what characteristic a certain day had, stubbornly persisting in extracting from the blurry sum a date to differentiate it. Not to live like a machine amidst the daily shuffle and the knitting, longing for Saturday to come in order to eat the crumb of memories that was incapable of satiating her heart's craving for tenderness. To put an end to the sordidness surrounding her, with its disguise of "do as you wish, but . . . ," of meticulousness, of concealed vigilance. To be no more. Never again to return to the house and find herself reporting what she had done and what it had yielded, listening to the insinuation regarding what had to be bought and what needed to be earned. To not get calluses on her hands pounding wheat, neither with her eyes weepy from the smoke of the oven, nor feeling her midsection aching in front of the laundry tub. Never to take pains with painting a little board and making a shelf, nor wallpapering the rooms, bedecking them with flowers like an imitation garden. Never. Nor ever again to feel him heaved over on top of her, panting and sweaty, heavy and without awakening any sensation in her other than a passive repugnance. Never.

The injury, which the air was turning cold, ached like a long stab wound. She touched it and found within the blood a hard point. A piece of glass. A spike-sized sliver from a broken glass that had buried itself there during the struggle, she did not know when. With a sort of insensitivity to the pain, she wiggled it to pull it out. She let out a groan. But furious with herself, in an abrupt tug that ripped her flesh more deeply, she pulled it out and tossed it away.

The blood was running through her fingers, around her neck, over her breasts. All stained and sticky, she kept going. To vanish. But first to sob, to shout, to howl. The wind, with its gusts, seemed to push its way inside her through her open flesh and make the pain intolerable. Greater still, sharper than the other pain which was destroying her feeling. Suddenly the hand that was gripping the apron, still holding the broken records, opened up and everything tumbled out over the ground. She took a few more steps and then fell face down sobbing, the sounds of which the wind seized with its strong hand and scattered throughout the surrounding area.

It was as if the water of those clear eyes could at last be water. She had the sensation that her mouth was opening for her, and she felt the strange noises being hurled from her throat and the scorched eyelids and wrinkled forehead and the salt from her weeping. And a hand clutching the wound, violently painful, and the blood running between her fingers and a braid of hair that must surely be soaked through and dampening her back. She raised herself up on one elbow; she turned her head. And she gave a sharp cry because a breath made her face feel warm and something inhuman terrified her to the point of losing consciousness.

The dog alternated periodically between sniffing her noisily, licking her hands, and sitting down—with his head raised on high, his snout stretched out toward mysterious omens—to deliver a long howl to the moon. He licked her face when the woman came to, and she knew instantaneously that it was the dog, although she did not know where she was. She sat up suddenly, and also suddenly she remembered her immediate situation.

It was as if she had not lived it. So strange, so alien to her. Almost like the sensation of the nightmare that had just become submerged in her subconscious. Was she fleeing from a dream; was she returning from some reality? A movement, on trying to stroke the dog, who was circling around her uneasily, gave her the exact shape of the facts. She groaned and the dog sought out her face again. But she pushed it aside, forcing it to lie down beside her. She pressed on the wound, which was oozing blood again, burning her as if she were being scalded.

She could bleed to death. To remain as she was, still in the night, in the cordial proximity of the dog until her blood went draining away and with it her life, that abhorrent life that she did not want to preserve for the benefit of another. Eliminating it, she avenged her constant state of humiliation, the animosities that had accumulated wordlessly, the resentment of a frustrated existence. To remove herself from the midst of things so that solitude might be the punishment for the man who would not have anyone to work, to produce and give an accounting of deeds and thoughts; the machine for his pleasure would have vanished and he would have to pay dearly to find another one so perfect as she. Not to see him again. Never to put in front of him the medium-done meat and see him chew with his surprisingly white teeth. Nor to see his gaze becoming clouded over, when desire made him reach out his hand to her futilely elusive body. Not to know that he was tangled up in subterranean calculations: "You'll buy this, because this little sum of money is to be stashed away and used to buy whenever possible the Urriolas' field, who are deep in debt and will finally have to sell, yes; or the field belonging to Valladares' widow, who with so many kids is not going to prosper, and they're going to put it up for auction, for the mortgage payments. . ." Waiting like a vulture, patiently, for the moment to take off with the prey. Land. Everything in him was reduced to that. To sell. To negotiate. To bring in money. And buy land, land.

To be no more. To think no more. To feel how the blood was slipping away through her fingers, running stickily over her chest, collecting in her lap, dampening her thighs.

The dog whined softly now, more and more restless. The woman, all of a sudden, opened her eyes, which no longer held any water other than that of their own clear irises, and she came face to face with a truth: to die was also never again to take out the memories of the past, that treasure chest with its images of tenderness. Never again to remember. . . To remember what? And in a rapid and incoherent superposition of images, snatches of scenes, fragments of sentences, she saw her mother sitting in front of the big gate, she saw herself with her sisters arm in arm, she saw the doves flying through the fragrant air of the garden. She perceived so exactly the smell of the jasmines that she inhaled longingly. But other images appeared: Herself crying between the piano box and the pile of mattresses; herself silent in the night under the moon's medallion in the bottom of the water tank; herself in front of the mirror, pinning a sprig of basil and some carnations into her braids, because Easter was an obstinately hopeful time; herself with her face turned around by the laughter and her eyes snaring the green gaze that stirred up a timid pigeon in her chest, so warm, so tender, so absolutely alive, that the surprise for her hand was not finding it sweetly nested there. . . All of that, never again. To die was also to renounce all of that.

Suddenly she stood up. Her legs felt unstable and little particles were dancing before her eyes. She closed them tight. She forced herself to hold herself erect. And also firmly she pressed the apron to her face, for she did not want the blood to flow through the wound, for she did not want the blood to abandon her, for death to leave her like an outspread rag in the middle of the field, on top of the mustard weeds, abandoned in the blackness with only the dog's protective custody. She wanted life, she wanted her blood, the branchwork of her blood, laden with memories.

She pressed the apron even harder against her cheek. She stared keenly into the night. Then she called the dog. She took it by its collar. And she said:

"Let's go home," and she followed it into the darkness.

Translated by Elaine Dorough Johnson

Plaza Mauá

Clarice Lispector

The cabaret on Plaza Mauá was called The Erotica. And Luisa's stage name was Carla.

Carla was a dancer at The Erotica. She was married to Joaquim, who was killing himself working as a carpenter. And Carla "worked" at two jobs: dancing half nude and cheating on her husband.

Carla was beautiful. She had little teeth and a tiny waist. She was delicate throughout. She had scarcely any breasts, but she had well-shaped hips. She took an hour to make herself up: afterward, she seemed a porcelain doll. She was thirty but looked much younger.

There were no children. Joaquim and she couldn't get together. He worked until ten at night. She began work at exactly ten. She slept all day long.

Carla was a lazy Luisa. Arriving at night, when the time came to present herself to the public, she would begin to yawn, wishing she were in her nightgown in bed. This was also due to shyness. Incredible as it might seem, Carla was a timid Luisa. She stripped, yes, but the first moments of the dance, of voluptuous motion, were moments of shame. She only "warmed up" a few minutes later. Then she unfolded, she undulated, she gave all of herself. She was best at the samba. But a nice, romantic blues also turned her on.

She was asked to drink with the clients. She received a commission per bottle. She always chose the most expensive drinks. And she pretended to drink: but hers wasn't alcohol. The idea was to get the clients drunk and make them spend. It was boring talking with them. They would caress her, passing their hands over her tiny breasts. And she in a scintillating bikini. Beautiful.

Once in a while she would sleep with a client. She would take the money, keep it well hidden in her bra, and the next day she would buy some new clothes. She had clothes without end. She bought blue jeans. And necklaces. A pile of necklaces. And bracelets and rings.

Sometimes, just for variety's sake, she danced in blue jeans and without a bra, her breasts swinging among the flashing necklaces. She wore bangs and, using a black pencil, painted on a beauty mark close to her delicate lips. It was adorable. She wore long pendant earrings, sometimes, pearl, sometimes imitation gold.

In moments of unhappiness, she turned to Celsinho, a man who wasn't a man. They understood each other well. She told him her troubles, complained about Joaquim, complained about inflation. Celsinho, a successful transvestite, listened to it all and gave her advice. They weren't rivals. They each worked their own turf.

Celsinho came from the nobility. He had given up everything for his vocation. He didn't dance. But he did wear lipstick and false eyelashes. The sailors of Plaza Mauá loved him. And he played hard to get. He only gave in at the very end. And he was paid in dollars. After changing the money on the black market, he invested it in the Banco Halles. He was very afraid of growing old, destitute and forsaken. Especially since an old transvestite is a sad thing. He took two envelopes of powdered proteins a day for energy. He had large hips and, from taking so many hormones, he had acquired a facsimile of breasts. Celsinho's stage name was Moleirão.

Moleirão and Carla brought good money to the owner of The

Erotica. The smoke-filled atmosphere, the smell of alcohol. And the dance floor. It was tough being forced to dance with a drunken sailor. But what could you do. Everyone has his *métier*.

Celsinho had adopted a little girl of four. He was a real mother to her. He slept very little in order to look after the girl. And she lacked for nothing: she had only the best. Even a Portuguese nanny. On Sundays Celsinho took little Clareta to the zoo at the Quinta de Boa Vista. And they both ate popcorn. And they fed the monkeys. Little Clareta was afraid of the elephants. She asked: "Why do they have such big noses?"

Celsinho then told her a fantastic tale involving good fairies and bad fairies. Or else he would take her to the circus. And they would suck hard, clicking candies, the two of them. Celsinho wanted a brilliant future for little Clareta: marriage with a man of fortune, children, jewels.

Carla had a Siamese cat who looked at her with hard blue eyes. But Carla scarcely had time to take care of the creature: either she was sleeping, or dancing, or out shopping. The cat was named Leléu. And it drank milk with its delicate little red tongue.

Joaquim hardly saw Luisa. He refused to call her Carla. Joaquim was fat and short, of Italian descent. It had been a Portuguese woman neighbor who had given him the name of Joaquim. His name was Joaquim Fioriti. Fioriti? There was nothing flowerlike about him.

The maid who worked for Joaquim and Luisa was a wily black woman who stole whatever she could. Luisa hardly ate, in order to keep her figure. Joaquim drowned himself in minestrone. The maid knew about everything, but kept her trap shut. It was her job to polish Carla's jewelry with Brasso and Silvo. When Joaquim was sleeping and Carla working, this maid by the name of Silvinha, wore her mistress's jewelry. And she was kind of grayish-black in color.

This is how what happened happened.

Carla was confiding in Moleirão when she was asked to dance by a tall man with broad shoulders. Celsinho lusted after him. And he ate his heart out in envy. He was vindictive.

When the dance ended and Carla returned to sit down next to Moleirão, he could hardly hold in his rage. And, Carla, innocent. It wasn't her fault she was attractive. And, in fact, the big man appealed to her. She said to Celsinho:

"I'd go to bed with that one for free."

Celsinho said nothing. It was almost three in the morning. The Erotica was full of men and women. Many mothers and housewives went there for the fun of it and to earn a bit of pocket money.

Then Carla said:

"It's so good to dance with a real man."

Celsinho sprang:

"But you're not a real woman!"

"Me? How come I'm not?" said the startled girl, who, dressed that night in black, in a long dress with long sleeves, looked like a nun. She did this on purpose to excite those men who desired a pure woman.

"You," screamed Celsinho, "are no woman at all! You don't even know how to fry an egg! And I do! I do! I do!"

Carla turned into Luisa. White, bewildered. She had been struck in her most intimate femininity. Confused, staring at Celsinho who had the face of a witch.

Carla didn't say a word. She stood up, crushed her cigarette in the ashtray, and, without turning to anyone, abandoning the party at its height, she left.

On foot, in black, on the Plaza Mauá at three in the morning. Like the lowest of whores. Alone. Without recourse. It was true: she didn't know how to fry an egg. And Celsinho was more of a woman than she.

The plaza was dark. And Luisa breathed deeply. She looked at the lampposts. The plaza was empty.

And in the sky, the stars.

Translated by Alexis Levitin

The Open Letter

The Open Letter

Helena Araujo

Ugh!! Elvira could feel the air getting thicker, the lamps getting brighter, and the atmosphere closing in with each passing moment. It was a heavy silence, and now she was starting to feel dizzy trying to remember what Martine told her the day before about the OIT, a violation of Conventions 85 and 86, no, 87 and 89, regarding the question asked by the same reporter who had asked for the file with the testimony of the prisoner whose head had been covered with a quilt before she was clubbed and then hung by her wrists for several hours while being threatened and beaten. Her nipples were pricked in front of some hooded people who were forced to stand on one foot and make a 4-shape with the other leg, their wrists handcuffed between the space of the 4 formed by the position of their two legs, yes, that's right, and a student, now exiled in Mexico, had told how they had him in that position, too, and then they dragged him inside and put a helmet on him and started to hit him until he fell down again and again. In the stomach, from behind, one beat him while the other kicked him and another grabbed and pinched his nipples and another raised his arms from behind his back at the same time that they pulled his head backwards until. . .

They torture people! They can't deny it! Elvira wanted to scream it out to him. And yet, there she was sitting in that armchair, hair freshly done, wearing a very tight tailored suit, calling him Mr. President and offering to translate into French what His Excellency was about to say, with a voice that sounded like a record playing at the wrong speed.

"Theeeeere aaaaare nooooo poliiiiiticaaaaal priiiiiisoners."

Then, naturally, the approving smiles of the people sitting in the back of the room, people that looked attentively at the delegates from the Colombia Committee. Stupefied, Elvira looked at the silken, embroidered walls of that suite of the Intercontinental Hotel where there were four Swiss detectives, two Latin American ones, an officer from the Colombian army, one from the Colombian navy, and one little, bald, ruddy-faced Ambassador whose slightly trembling hands had revealed a certain discomfort with having run into her in the Hotel lobby: Elvirita, Elvirita, you're mixed up in *this?* Of course, because the Ambassador was Eugenio Vélez, and he had recognized her right away. It was impossible not to: after all, Medellin was Medellin. They had grown up on the same block of Poblado. Vélez had been her brother's best friend in high school and then in college; they even started their careers at the same time. The only difference was that Vélez got involved sooner in the Liberal Central Committee. That's probably why they made him Ambassador, as a reward for all the votes he brought in, right? Well, a lot of water had gone under the bridge since Elvira had last seen him or gone to Medellin to avoid the unpleasantness of also seeing her brother. She did know, however, that both he and Eugenio Vélez had done some very fast climbing. Of course, it was to be expected from a couple of ass-licking, two-faced squealers like them. That's exactly what Elvira had screamed at her brother the last time he had the nerve to warn her, with his first-born-male voice and inquisitorial airs, that getting involved with "those people" was disrespectful to the memory of their dead parents. Amen. So be it. That day Elvira felt like grabbing him by the collar of his pink shirt and pulling on the knot of his striped tie until he screamed. But instead, patience, she answered him slowly, gritting her teeth, that she simply believed in defending Human Rights. This happened more than five years ago. Meanwhile, Elvira traveled, got married. And now, she could expect Eugenio Vélez would communicate to her brother that even in Switzerland she was mixed up with "those people." So much the better. And even congratulate him on his marriage to that stupid wealthy woman whom he'd married just to get to be the manager of Coltejer.

Ugh! When Ambassador Vélez advanced toward her smiling, Elvira made a face as if she were suffering from heartburn. Then, in French, she introduced him to the people from the CRT and the VPOD and the FOBB, as well as to other union leaders, seven in all, who did not respond, and to Martine, unsmiling, in a yellow dress that made her look taller and skinnier than usual, although Elvira had lent her an Indian necklace so that with her blonde hair she wouldn't look like she was all of one color. When Martine got serious like that you could see that her face was as furrowed as the wood carvings that made the region where she was born so famous. Valais, she was one solemn Valaissian woman. Still, Elvira was glad she had dressed the way she did, and she in her dark suit, because the union people all came without ties except the two bearded ones with trenchcoats who reread the letter many times before the slight silhouette of Ambassador Vélez appeared on the first step of the escalator beside an individual who was probably his bodyguard judging from the Rocky Marciano action and the authority with which Vélez ordered him to say right beside him while he went to greet "those people." That's when he came out with *Elvirita-Elvirita.* Eugenio Vélez probably would have kept up the *Elvirita* business in the elevator if she hadn't developed a sudden formal interest in the menu of the day, posted at the extreme opposite from the corner where he continued warning photographers that they couldn't take pictures.

Two minutes later, when she entered the suite on the eleventh floor, the Ambassador announced a Colombian woman, Mr. President, from Antioquia, Mr. President, and sister of the manager of Coltejer. Ugh! When Elvira went in and saw him in that arm chair in the back of the room next to a small table that held a chalet made of chocolate, no doubt a gift from Nestlé's, she had the sensation that he wasn't really the President. She couldn't believe it: he looked like an enormous, voluminous puppet, a straw figure, like some animal stuffed with cotton waste or foam rubber, sewn up and planted there in that green velvet arm chair. Confused, Elvira tried to move forward. It was difficult for her to stand up, stop, extend her hand, and shake those tepid, pudgy fingers. Meanwhile, Martine and the others imitated her gesture, forming a semi-circle. Now Elvira would have to listen, translate, repeat what, with so much effort, the President was starting to say. In truth, the words seemed to come out of that moist mouth so painfully. The President's eyes were concentrating on some fixed point that his thick glasses made impossible to determine; his voluminous body was covered in dark blue fabric, his head harder and more stylized than his body, which was apparently missing joints and cartilage. Yes, everything about him seemed like a flabby succession of folds, seams and creases: his tightly-buttoned jacket, his pants covering those flat knees, his hands at his sides, slightly wrinkled, as if they hadn't filled out enough.

Strangely, when the President began to speak, it seemed to Elvira that he was not expressing himself of his own initiative, but rather that he was controlled by some other force, as if he were a ventriloquist's dummy. You could say that someone, far away, was dictating those slow, hesitant sentences, someone who also controlled the movement of those hands, kept the cheeks of that face inflated, and maintained the posture of that flaccid body. It was true: his voice seemed guided by remote control. Hesitatingly, Elvira had to concentrate to keep up with the translation. His accent seemed to prolong the vowels; it tired her and made her drowsy. Sometimes she thought she heard a kind of muffled groan dying away, like an echo. There were other times when she heard a purring, a buzzing. She was almost always sure that she was repeating in French. The Spanish sounded as if it were already being repeated. Finally, she started to feel sleepy, her eyelids so heavy she asked herself whether she was too tired to continue. It was probably the accumulated fatigue of the last few days that was catching up with her. Not eating regular meals, lack of sleep. The night before she had gone to bed late again after Martine had brought her home with Pacho and Socorro in the wee hours of the morning after the last meeting. As usual, El Flaco had given her a hard time, bawling her out, his blue eyes getting bigger and bigger as he blurted out guttural obscenities in Spanish. As usual, Elvira just shrugged her shoulders, telling him that *he* was the exhausted one, slouching more every day, while his athletic gait turned into some kind of sleepwalking. Then, worn out and irritated, he showed her what he had for her, a surprise, something that had occurred to him that evening when he was drawing pictures for Chelita and explaining Colombian politics to her. Trying to hide her laughter, Elvira admired the caricature: a fat round man wearing a kepi on one side of his head and a high hat on the other: on one side a bowtie and on the other epaulets, eyes staring into space, and under them an enormous smile. Each tooth was separated by a prison bar behind which torture victims and prisoners were struggling. It would make a great poster. When Elvira said so, instead of telling her to go right to bed El Flaco invited her to sit down and have a cup of coffee with him in the kitchen. The black liquid was hot and they slowly sipped it, talking about the press conference and how the reporters tired of waiting for the Jesuit priest and the Union teacher because Roger couldn't find them anywhere in the Geneva terminal and Elvira had had to get angry, call him stubborn, and swear to him that it was those two over there next to the door of the second class cafeteria, because in spite of his beard and his blue jeans, he was a priest, and beside him was Socorro, the one with the curly hair and the glasses. Elvira recognized her from when they had met in the Federation of Antioquia and Elvira would have gone on telling El Flaco for the thousandth time just how and when and where and with whom, if El Flaco hadn't cursed and left the kitchen advising her to take a good look in the mirror at those bags under her eyes, and turning out the light immediately so she'd be compelled to go to sleep. Now Elvira would evoke, as in mirage, the mattresses on the living room floor of their small apartment in the midst of that mess of ashtrays and leftover food, the sticky sensation of having stayed awake all night. Martine and Pacho and Socorro asleep with their clothes on while she and El Flaco together on the divan, each lying as if alone, exhausted, in a deep sleep until the next bell rang.

"Rrriiiiiiiiing!"

The first call was at seven from the Socialist Party: then the Protestant Social Center called while they were having breakfast. Next CARITAS, then a round of TVB, ADTP, SEV, OCLDR followed by the FTMH and the FSCG. For the first time Elvira had gotten all those initials straight while she took frantic notes and Pacho and Socorro applauded, helping to wash the dishes. It was like a marathon, like playing auction. By 8:00 a.m. there were fifty-five signatures, by 8:30 fifty-eight, by 9:00 sixty-three, by 9:30 sixty-seven, at 10:00 seventy and at 11:00 seventy-four. Roger classified everything, bending his head forward and smiling with that cunning little look that made so many people ask if he wasn't from Antioquia instead of Switzerland. There were the lists of labor unions, political parties, humanitarian institutions and so many other columns that the old Remington just went on lining up without even skipping the spaces where the springs were missing, because El Flaco knew just the trick to keep it from jamming and he was the one who was finishing the job while Roger went to put gas in the van that Martine would pilot again at 90 kms an hour with Chelita at her side asking why so fast.

In the end, the only ones who went to Geneva were Chelita, Elvira and Martine because Socorro had some other important business to take care of. Well, Pacho went too, and it's a good thing because he took care of Chilita and calmed Elvira who was unnerved by the delay. All right already, they explained to her a thousand times that they couldn't leave until the phone calls from all the labor unions were answered and the list of signatures was complete and Elvira pleaded with them, repeating that it was crazy to wait, they should have left sooner, that they'd never get to Geneva by 12, especially considering that they didn't even know where the

Intercontinental Hotel was. When they actually made it to Geneva by 12 in spite of the rain and Highway Patrol, Elvira made Martine stop at the corner, opened the door, eagerly jumped out and stopped at least three people who all signaled first to the right and then to the left to explain where the Intercontinental Hotel was. Finally, the van started up with a hiccough and as soon as they saw a glass tower with an enormous parking lot, Elvira got out again, slamming the door, telling Martine to get there fast and Pacho to take care of Chelita, we'll meet at the café in the Station in an hour.

Well, at this point, maybe Elvira didn't realize that her resistance had been wearing down and surely by now she was quite weak as she reclined against a console in a corner of that lobby that looked like an airport (escalators and neon lights) but furnished in nouveau-riche style and occupied by people with dark skin and expensive clothes and among whom she couldn't find those other people with the light skin and used clothing who were the labor union leaders from VPOD and CRT and FOBB and all those other initials that got on her nerves. Really, for all her cursing and grumpiness, she hadn't even noticed a group of people next to the parking lot booth, standing in the light, persistent rain that had made the highway so slippery. In fact, it was so very slippery that Elvira couldn't imagine how they'd arrived on time, with Martine like a racing-car driver, avoiding the radar traps to swallow up all those kilometers in just twenty minutes and arrive at the appointed time only to find that the representatives from the Swiss labor unions weren't there yet. Damn them! But, the truth was that they were there: it's just that Elvira and Martine had passed them by too quickly because they were such nervous wrecks. That was it. They hadn't even noticed that group of people without an umbrella, shaking rain off their feet and cursing the bad weather. When Martine finally discovered them, got out and called them, Elvira started to clap and shout and Martine herself was acting much more scandalous than any other woman from Valais in similar circumstances. Honestly. They made such a ruckus in the lobby that fortunately the Ambassador had that 15-minute delay which gave them time to sit down, reread the letter, count the signatures one more time, comment on the lousy weather and observe indifferently the slim and tidy appearance of someone who appeared at the top of the escalator, slowly descending flanked by a bodyguard.

Who knows. Maybe it was precisely Ambassador Vélez' compassionate greeting, with that look that seemed to say, "Honey, what are you involved in?" that Elvira found most irritating. Or maybe it was Martine's impatience when Vélez said no photographers because two of them from Interpress had appeared with cameras and refused to comply with the Ambassador's order, who in turn refused to allow them to go any farther so nobody could document the zeal with which four male gorillas and one female one searched the bags and pockets of the Colombia Committee delegation who had asked for an audience with His Excellency, Mr. President, to hand deliver an Open Letter protesting the repression. In any case, those people got their way and got in there even though the Ambassador had refused to receive them and the Colombian Mission at first, and everyone acted like they forgot about it until Martine warned them by phone that unless they had the audience, they would create a scandal with the press. They must certainly have believed it when the next day *La Gazette* and *Le Courrier* and *La Tribune*—and every other newspaper published—prefaced the already short news item about the arrival of Monsieur le President de la Colombie with two long paragraphs about an Open Letter that would be delivered to him from a Solidarity Committee denouncing the house breakings, arrests and torture.

"Theeeeee neeeeeews paaaaapers coooooment..."

Elvira had started to translate the sentence, controlling her anger and gutturalizing as much as possible, trying to avoid the gaze of the man in uniform who had taken his place right in front of her, most likely to be able to watch them closely, to observe her and Martine, in all probability for closer identification. Yes, so he could give a detailed account of their faces and general appearance in case they tried to travel to Colombia and then nab them. Suddenly Elvira wondered how he would describe them. For example, tall, flat-chested blonde with busty, short brunette. One born in 'forty-eight and the other in 'forty-six. Married to Swiss men. Profession: Social workers. From Antioquia and Valais, prosperous Catholic regions of two distant countries. Then again—and what would stop him?—the man in uniform might be much more imaginative, more eloquent. He might like certain variations. For example, Martine was bony and angular with molasses-colored hair, freckled and eyes that turned greener each time she asked the President questions. There was that, and each time he answered apathetically, Martine would first frown and then her eyes would shine and her teeth would show even though she was trying to suppress her laughter. Yes, slouching over like a humpback, like a little girl afraid of being reprimanded. Elvira, on the other hand, was tall and erect, but also muscular with a tendency to get round in those places where her body was like those clay pots that acquired a better color after being fired because her skin was dark, though her face was paler, maybe in contrast with her black eyes and eyebrows, or with her abundant hair which, in vain, she always had to swear was her natural color, the same way she was always assuring people that she hadn't had her teeth capped, those teeth that were as surprising for their whiteness as for their sharpness, excellent, for example for cutting rope or gnawing at chicken bones.

"The letter, Mr. President. . ."

This time the hurried, sharp watchful voice came from the Ambassador. He had spoken and his hands were shaking again as they folded the letter while His Excellency was saying that those present had come to inform him of unknoooooown faaaaaacts. Yes, it was as if they knew about the letter beforehand without having even read it, so Elvira did not have the pleasure of quoting the report on the jails, nor the number of people organized in the movement against the Statute of Security, right? No. Elvira could not quote any of it. The letter, typed by El Flaco and signed by seventy-four Swiss organizations, just sat there on the table that was in front of the couch where the Ambassador was sitting, to the right of the President and to the left of a print easy-chair where Elvira remained, numb and stupefied, trying to translate what seemed like a broadcast from a transistor radio with dead batteries.

"An aaaaaaarmy looooooyal tooo the Cooooonstituuuuution. . ."

Now his speech became more and more hesitant, although it was supposedly the most decisive moment of the audience, the reason for giving it in the first place. That must be it, the President had received them so he could hear his own voice. Even though he spoke in slow motion. Besides, he hadn't paid the slightest attention to the contents of the Open Letter nor to the questions he was asked. Rumor had it that he understood French, but whenever one of the labor leaders asked him a question in that language, he answered something that had nothing to do with the question. Or else he sat there silently as if half-asleep, without paying any attention to what was being asked, with his gaze fixed at some point on which his thick glasses focused beyond Elvira, Martine and that Swiss lake landscape hanging on an embroidered wall. But now, now he was talking and everyone was smoking like a chimney in that room with hermetically-sealed windows supposedly designed for air-conditioning, and this too contributed to Elvira's discomfort. Each time she tried to translate, the words seemed to fade away, to get lost in a kind of nasal monotony as if they were echoing that same voice with which the President was inviting the esteemed citizens of Switzerland here today to visit his country, to see with their own eyes theeeeee deomoooooo-craaaacy that preeeeeevaiiiiled there. Exhausted, Elvira repeated the phrase with a hesitant intonation, as if her spirit were faltering. Well, surely she would have capitulated, she would have gone to pieces, even fainted, if she hadn't seen those two pudgy hands on the arms of the chair and heard a straining thrust as they turned purple under the stress of supporting all that weight.

Yes, it was then that they heard Martine clearing her throat, her eyes getting greener, who was looking at the His Excellency, telling him in her improvised Spanish: "President. I accept invitation travel to Colombia. Want to see Modelo, Picota and Sacromonte prisons."

Then another silence. Strained at first, and then letting up, as if something were slowly deflating. Elvira noticed that one of the union people wisely covered his mouth while the other smiled quite openly. With that, the people in the back stood up, and then the one from the CRT and the FOBB and then the one from CMI also stood up, and all the others followed suit. Then Elvira finally stood up also, straightening herself out with an awkward gesture, opening her eyes wide and looking around as if she'd just emerged from the dark. Only then did her anxiety and nervousness seem to return as she looked for the door and rapidly walked toward it, in such a hurry to get out that she left Martine and the others behind. She was leaving without hearing Vélez' little voice nagging at her, thanking her for the translation, *Elvirita, thanks for the French, Elvirita*, with that clammy hand and that handshake before the elevator door opened.

The others who were right behind didn't get there in time to get into the elevator with Elvira and had to wait for the next one. Nevertheless, when they finally did reach ground level, she was nowhere to be found in the hotel lobby. Thinking that she had gone to pick Chelita up at the station cafeteria, they headed there; again no Elvira. They also checked with some other friends with no luck. Then they thought she might have had an accident, but no hospital or emergency room had admitted her. Finally, rather alarmed, Roger and Martine called El Flaco. After two days of searching and insomnia, he finally received a note marked "urgent" sent from the airport which read: "I'm going to Colombia. Take good care of Chelita. I don't know whether or not I'm coming back."

For Mariela and Marie-Claire
Lausanne
July-August 1979

Translated by Nancy Saporta Sternbach

Cecilia's Last Will and Testament

Alicia Steimberg

I found these papers on top of the piano, in the house where Cecilia lived for so many years, after she had already left. I had the keys to the house and used them to get in after nobody answered the bell. It was a summer night. The window was open, letting in a sultry breeze that smelled of the earth and promised a storm.

I always thought that people who write their last wills and testaments do it because they feel that death is near, be it from old age, from an incurable disease, execution or suicide. As you will see, Cecilia was not facing any of these. I suppose that she was merely thinking about her death. Or perhaps about the death of an era, of a part of her life.

The storm ceased to be a threat and became a real storm: the wind whipped the curtains on the windows and the leaves of the trees in the garden, and rain pattered down, a delight to hear from the apartment. I sat in Cecilia's armchair, lit a lamp, and began to read.

*   *   *

Buenos Aires/January, 1978

I want to set down here my last will and testament. I have no idea as to how these things are supposed to be written, but I am sure that whoever finds these pages will take the trouble to contact my heirs and carry out my wishes. I don't believe it should be necessary to undertake any legal proceedings. Nonetheless, I have made certain arrangements as regards particular matters, such as my burial. I will begin with my testament.

To Pepe, I leave the last ten years of my life, with their corresponding pleasures and pains (more pains than pleasure, Pepe would say). However, and he knows it, these were not the worst years of my life. Quite the contrary. The last two or three in particular were without question the best. I came to feel so satisfied with things that an epitaph occurred to me. It does not appear among these things here willed because, on account of a remark Pepe made, I changed my mind and decided not to use it. After the conventional "Here lies...," the inscription I had in mind said: "Do not be sad. Or, if you must, be sad, but know that in life I did what I wanted to do." Pepe looked at me pityingly and said:

"They'll kick the stone over."

He feels it's preferable not to show too much happiness over nothing to avoid making others envious.

To Francisco, whom I stopped seeing so long ago I can hardly remember him, but with whom I also shared a number of years of my life, I leave that unforgettable dream about the Chacarita. More than a cemetery, the place seemed like the Edwardian interior of the Molino Café. At the counter there was a fat man counting money; in the following scene I found myself in a place that looked more like a cemetery, beneath a dome supported by columns. From the roof of the dome there was a thin tube of rubber suspended. As I drew close to see what it was, a torrent of money came out of the tube, while a voice echoed down from above, saying: "Let's say forty-six to keep it twenty-seven."

I have no notion what those numbers mean: I leave the problem to Francisco. It may not be very nice to bequeath a problem to someone, but he left me a number of them, and I had no say as to whether I accepted them or not. On the other hand, nobody is obligated to take something left to him in a will. He can keep it or throw it in the trash, or donate it to charity.

To Sergio, who has stuck by me unfailingly for nearly twenty years, and who never abandoned me, I leave all the moments of freedom from my life, but especially one night when I opened an exquisite box of French-perfumed body powder (this is quite an extraordinary bequest, because it was the only time in my life that I used body powder), and then went to meet him. I wish I recalled whether we got drunk or just a little tipsy. What Sergio should know is that I was happy that night, because it was important to him, and still is important to him, that I am happy.

To José, I leave all my literary prowess, in honor of the heroic enthusiasm with which he embraced my first efforts. I say heroic because, knowing José, it's impossible to imagine him showing enthusiasm for anything. It took all the cunning I could muster to find out that behind the profound melancholy of his face, that aqueous, funereal gaze that seems to set a stone on whatever it touches, there was enthusiasm, I would say almost great enthusiasm for those early pirouettes of mine. José is such a pessimist that he doesn't believe in anything in the future. Every time he announces something, he adds:

"If nothing happens. . . If something doesn't come up. . . There are always those unforseen kinds of things. . ." And a terrifying silence falls in which anyone would start to doubt everything.

José's childhood is an absolute secret, but I'm sure that horrifying things happened to him and he prefers not to remember. Maybe he was hungry; maybe they beat him with a whip; maybe they shut him up in a dark, windowless room.

Just in case, I leave him as well my recurrent fantasy that I am locked in a kind of safe made of stainless steel, like a modern bank under construction might have. The safe is quite spacious, with no right angles: the joints of the walls with the roof and floor are all rounded. It is hermetically sealed, impregnable, but I know I will be held there only for a limited number of hours. I must remain calm, I think, tomorrow they'll come to take me out of here. All things considered, the best thing I can do is sleep. I lay down on the stainless steel floor; I try to find a comfortable position and can't. The worst thing is that the space is lit, and I don't really know where the light's coming from. Finally, I curl up on my side and open my eyes. If they are open, I have to look at the steel walls, and I'm very frightened. I'm incapable of thinking of absolutely anything, of filling my head with whatever, like I can in everyday situations. Ideas, memories, random thoughts, imagined conversations with different people, everything empties out of my head like water through a colander. I have a brain full of stainless steel; I close my eyes again and trying counting to a hundred. If I make it to a hundred I will sleep; and I will only wake up when they open the door to let me out of here. But, really, why am I here? Am I trying to rob the bank? Or did I wander in here by mistake, distracted, thinking it was an elevator, and then it shut automatically behind me until ten o'clock next morning? I can't remember why I'm here, and the terror reaches a point that I decide to abandon this particular fantasy, and replace it with other, more pleasant thoughts.

I leave this fantasy to José. From the perennial torment he wears on his face, I figure he'll know what to do with it. Besides, I'm leaving on a trip and don't have room for much useless baggage.

To Silvana I leave my spotty wardrobe. She, like me, suffers from that peculiar lack of confidence in any outfit not consisting of designer blue jeans and a plaid shirt. With my closet, she won't have to shudder before diaphanous dresses or high-heeled sandals. I always wanted them, and only now that I'm leaving this house forever can I permit myself to buy them.

To Matilde I leave the tremendous collection of uninhibited screeching I kept boxed up year to year, ever since she started to lay that kind of thing on me. I never knew why I saved any, given that it was made up almost entirely of reproaches, insults, and bitter complaints about her own unhappiness, for which I honestly believed myself somehow responsible. It was with considerable surprise that I realized that Matilde would have been miserable even without me, because misery is her profession and her destiny. Maybe

I saved all that yelling so I could return it to her sometime. It might give her a certain satisfaction to remember. It would be nice if Matilde recalled that when I was first the object of that yelling I was only a little girl, and some of that I wasn't able to stuff into the box I'm leaving her. Some echoes eternally my ears. I also leave her a rare moment of calm in which I, with the innocence appropriate to my tender years, believed in a lasting peace between the two of us. We were walking together, one sunny afternoon, along the Avenida Juan B. Justo. We came to a humble little house with a wooden door painted blue. Matilde rang the bell and a fat, freckled woman with bright red cheeks opened the door, revealing a long corridor of black and white tile. Matilde and the woman exchanged a few words I didn't hear. I was absorbed in the tiles of the corridor and in a chicken coop I could see in the back. The woman left us waiting, clumped heavily down the hallway, and opened the wire door of the chicken coop, causing great confusion among the birds. She soon returned with something wrapped in her apron: three recently laid eggs. Matilde allowed me to carry them in a little paper bag. They were warm. Back at home, we whipped one of those eggs with port and sugar. I drank the heavy mixture in great gulps and felt a pleasant warmth and a light sleepiness. A brief happiness, and the illusion that it would last forever.

To Eduardo, I leave the poems of incomprehensible words we composed between the two of us; it was he who said that in them we had captured our madness, so we might look at it fearlessly in the dark days of our infancy. Thank God we had each other. It wasn't long ago that somebody ran into us at a party and asked if we'd been introduced.

"Not exactly," I said. The first time they presented me to Eduardo, he refused to recognize my presence, did not reply to my hello, nor pay me any attention at all.

Surprised, the mutual friend who had wanted to introduce us remained silent. Then I explained to him that when I was presented to Eduardo, he was in a cradle in the maternity ward of the hospital.

Our friend laughed, but I don't know if he really thought the joke was all that funny. I think he finds me a bit complicated, but

I always have to find something that distracts me from the horror of being buried alive in that safe made of stainless steel.

To Marisa, I leave all those songs we sang till dawn in harmony when we were twenty, especially "By the Bridge, Janey," which went "By the bridge, Janey, not by the stream." We conjectured about that phrase, and reached the conclusion that if Janey went by the bridge she'd keep living, whereas if she went by the stream she'd drown. We might have come up with other notions, for example, what if Janey could swim, but we were fixated on the idea of suicide and suicides seemed very interesting. Around this time a friend of Marisa shot herself in the heart and lived. Marisa respected her almost to the point of veneration, as did I, because I based my sentiments on Marisa's, given I couldn't copy her seductiveness, her beauty, or her utter disregard for everybody in the world except herself. I never met the suicide, and I may have had some different ideas about her, but I was very careful not to let on so Marisa wouldn't make fun of me. I leave her as well that kind of fun, carefully classified and labelled as: wounding phrases, deprecatory glances directed at me, deprecatory glances directed at others and shared with me, the way she could curve those beautiful lips in a rictus of disgust, the toe-pointing practiced when she had one leg crossed over the other. She will find them in a box that originally contained sandalwood soap, a masculine aroma she liked so well, hidden beneath a tiny reproduction of a work by her beloved Chagall.

I know that it is unusual to leave things to someone already dead, but the next time somebody goes to put flowers of Ignacio's grave, please put along with them all the ingenious or intelligent phrases I ever said that he always used to marvel aloud at. With that, he managed to convince me early on that I was quite an exceptional sort, with unique gifts. The blows of life (why not) have busied themselves convincing me that if, indeed, I am able to make invisible cats scamper across roofs drawn out of air, for many other things, I'm a hopeless idiot, something Ignacio would never have admitted. Also put on his tomb a leaf from a children's book that I read over and over when I was small. It talked about honey, and showed a bee, a honeycomb, a jar of honey, and a boy sitting at a table, spreading honey on a piece of bread. The text spoke of the various applications of honey, and whenever I read this page I remembered Ignacio, who was so fond of me and never yelled at me, and who so shortly after left this world that an incurable astonishment remained with me ever since.

Ana: To you, who certainly will find these pages on top of the piano, I leave everything you find in this house, from the furniture to the ghosts, and including the contents of various drawers. Study each letter carefully, every photograph. Don't be alarmed if, upon opening a door, you feel suddenly like you've gone back thirty years. This house was remodeled several times, and in the back there is a patio of uneven tiles, a bath, an unused kitchen, full of old appliances and cookware, and a tiny room with a very small window separate from all the other bedrooms. When I was little I desperately wished that that were my room, but I would never have dared suggest it. When the servant girl had a bed, it was her room. When she didn't, it was the ironing room. But it was a refuge to which I could flee for brief periods. There you will find many of my dreams and adolescent fantasies, a photo of Carlos Gardel, and a wave of violent perfume that its last occupant slathered herself with to go out on Sundays. They are all yours, Ana.

It embarrasses me to give away old knick-knacks, but maybe you will find among all the trash in the back of the house a little shelf that once hung on the dining room wall, with the following miniatures on it: a Lilliputian edition in two volumes of *Don Quixote*, a free gift from Escasany Jewelers, bound in Russian leather and printed on onionskin, that includes only the chapter about the windmills, and a little, very fat bronze doll called Billiken, that had some sort of importance as an amulet.

From the old bathroom, you might want to take: "Life offers three great gifts: health, wealth, and love..." and "Sorrento" in the rendition of Aunt Rosita who sang it every time she took a shower. Also, my face as a girl reflected in the mirror of the medicine chest, and the tube of mascara with which Matilde used to blacken her lashes every morning in an act mechanical as brushing her teeth. Also, the extreme cruelty of her eyes as she applied the mascara.

Finally, in that closed up kitchen there is a pile of children's books full of educational and macabre stories, like the one about the unfortunate girl who lodged some poor relatives in her house, who ended up poisoning her, and who, as she writhed around in her death throes, repented of their crime and so *confessed it all to her.* And the dying girl was so, so very good that she managed to forgive them all before rocketing off to Heaven.

When you make your pass through the modernized part of the house, notice that in the bathroom there are a number of toothbrushes, more than there were ever people in the house. Every time that I picked up my toothbrush I was amazed at the presence of all those anonymous toothbrushes. I would be completely absorbed, nearly hypnotized, by my own inability to remember where they came from. However, I never got around to throwing them all away, as if I were afraid of loosing some curse. There's a very old one of antique design that looks like it was used to clean dentures, and that always drew forth a particular repugnance from me. But I wasn't even capable of tossing that one out. What will you do with all those toothbrushes, Ana? And with all the liqueur glasses up on the top shelf in the kitchen? Maybe you can use one for eyebaths, like Gramma did. She filled the little glass with some mysterious liquid and then—pop!—she planted it with one quick, agile movement over her eye. One nice thing about Gramma was that she didn't mind me sitting there looking at her with my mouth open when she pressed an empty bottle of cod liver oil to her face. Through the remnants of the liquid and the glass, her eye acquired extraordinary dimensions, and after she had held it there for a while she smiled at me, triumphant, and I looked at her, fascinated.

In the back of the closets are shoes, Ana, the kind I ought to have thrown out years ago, but they're still there. I don't think they'll be of interest to anybody. I ask only that you take them up on the balcony of the top floor and throw them, aiming as best you can, into the vacant lot in front. For years I lived in this house complaining bitterly of the antisocial monsters who threw things in the vacant lot. I accused them of being mentally defective. I never did anything like that. But now I want to give myself the chance, even if it's by proxy. One old shoe, another, another, ready, aim, fire.

As for the rest, you can decide its destiny, except for the piano that I will have sent to my new house. I never knew how to play, but it's a memento of Aunt Rosita who could only play "Fuer Elise."

And now, my Last Request:

I want to be buried without ceremony (though I wouldn't mind flowers, which I've always liked) in the cemetery of the Chacarita in Buenos Aires. I have always lived in Buenos Aires, and the Chacarita is Buenos Aires. It has its ugly neighborhoods, and its pretentious ones, the prettier neighbors where the members of certain of the foreign communities live, or die, or are dead. There are the walls of niches, with the dead piled up just like the living in apartment houses. People choose the place they want, or that they can afford, within the cemetery.

Never bring calla lilies, I hate them. Nor carnations, nor jonquils, which are funeral flowers. I like roses, jasmine, sweet peas.

I declare that in the moment of this writing I am in good health, I work hard, and am looking forward to enjoying life.

Cecilia

As I finished reading, I noticed the rain had stopped. I leaned out the window to think. I had never met any of the people that Cecilia mentioned in her will, so it would be impossible for me to parcel out her inheritance. To comply with her last wishes, I would need legal authorization, that supposing, of course, that Cecilia died before I did, something utterly unpredictable. As far as I know, she never had family, except her grandmother who died long ago; Aunt Rosita must have been some invention of hers.

She actually always wanted relatives. She was fascinated, almost hypnotized when she spoke to me about the secretaries that take the buses out to the suburbs every afternoon, and, arriving at their humble homes, find an old mother, bent, a shawl she's crocheted herself over her shoulders, who has dinner waiting. Then she would go on to describe the dinner, and her face would take on the vagueness of delirium. Dinner was invariably prepared with leftovers: stew from the roast, bread-pudding with scraps from the whole week. The mother and her daughter moved from room to room over the slick floor on scuffs made of wool scraps. Night after night, the two together ate those meals made from leftovers. The problem, the insoluble enigma that cost Cecilia more than one sleepless night, was what the original meal had been, the one that provided the first leftovers. But Cecilia was sufficiently sensitive to turn away from that dead end. Just as she slipped out of that stainless steel safe without anybody's having come to open the door, she circled around the quiche made with last night's greens, and spent half-an-hour thinking about surfing.

"It's a sport that now I'll never have a chance to take up, and I regret it," she said.

She admired the bronzed, triumphant bodies shooting across the crest of a wave. Surfing was the symbol of all she had never done or known in her life. When a physicist tried to explain the notion of the infinite in terms utterly incomprehensible to her, she shook her head sadly and said:

"That and surfing, no chance."

She was tough-minded about her limitations, and I think she exaggerated them.

But I don't know why I'm talking about Cecilia as if she were dead. It's that eccentricity of hers that drove her to make out this will.

I will take these pages with me. They have no legal value and Cecilia won't be able to be buried as she wishes until we find the. . . But this has to be handled delicately. It doesn't seem particularly nice to hurry things along where a case like this is concerned. Besides, I don't know when I'll see her next, since she says she's not coming back. But I know she'll be back. As long as I live, Cecilia will be back.

Translated by Christopher Leland

The Compulsive Couple of the House on the Hill

Carmen Naranjo

When they met, he set out the conditions explicitly. Marriage is a serious commitment, especially when you're ambitious and power-hungry; besides, you're already accustomed to a certain lifestyle and aren't looking for change, and as if that were not enough, marriage is a tricky business, because when it is a question of catching the fish, everything is just fine and only afterwards come the complaints, protests, grudges and infinite bitching.

The day was dark and it was barely two o'clock in the afternoon. The dense air hung heavily, in spite of the open windows and the raucous fan that snored with the rhythm of dry heaves. He was sweating moderately; she profusely, flushed with the heat and the anguish that was written all over her face. I'm not one of those women who's fickle and I love you and I will always love you just the same. My only concern will be to please you, to please you in every way, even when I don't know how, I will never complain, never. You wouldn't mistrust me if you knew me better.

Outside, the noisy birds were lamenting the rain and it wasn't even raining that day. It rained for the wedding, a year and a half later. She arrived first, with only the relatives that he had invited because he didn't think all of them were suitable. Not her carpenter uncle and his family because they were gluttons and stupid; not her cousins from that detestable dusty town because they were ignorant and they embraced you too enthusiastically and anyway they smelled of bologna; not her brothers in-law because they were ugly and because the way they had of laughing betrayed their imbecility.

She arrived, serene and pale. No one noticed the slight trembling of her left hand. Her white, chiseled face would have revealed even to the casual observer a year and a half of confinement, a year and a half of complying with instructions that were increasingly stringent, increasingly severe, a year and a half of silence because she had learned to say only what he wanted to hear, a year and a half without girlfriends, whom she was losing one by one because you give your heart to me completely, leaving no room for anyone else and from now on I am your father, your mother and your whole life.

He arrived half an hour later, the impertinent rain and his torn pants having kept him, not to mention the folly of so many people participating in an act as stupid as a wedding.

The ceremony was longer than it had to be and uncomfortable, because he grunted several times and tapped his foot repeatedly, as if he thought it necessary to retort: pure foolishness this stuff the priest is saying because he doesn't even know what the matrimonial yoke is.

When they left, after the rain had slackened to an inoffensive drizzle, he elbowed her to look at the hill: there we will have a house up high and when I'm mayor I'll wave to the people from the balcony. She said that yes, it would be a lovely house, and that she was already dreaming about caring for it meticulously so that he would be happy and feel utterly proud. He replied that everything would be his decision and done to suit his tastes.

It is said that they were deeply happy. He always walked in front of her on their walks from exactly six-thirty until seven-forty-five on the dot. Precisely two steps in front. Each night she seemed a little smaller, as if she were shrinking. Perhaps it was a simple optical illusion; perhaps it was the hunched-over posture with which she combined her short steps.

They built their house high on top of the hill. White with a red roof. The balcony presided over a simple architecture of symmetrical windows and, perpendicular to the balcony, a narrow door with a bronze door-knocker.

Things went well for them in their business dealings. He had an instinct for opportunity and prices; she was thrifty, with a passion for efficiency, constant work and taking advantage of things that on the surface seemed useless. Their assets grew with the purchase of a supermarket, then a bookstore with a little printing press in the rear and finally a hardware store with a repair shop for those machines now known as appliances.

Of course they did have problems managing their employees. He dictated a moral and behavioral code, replete with duties and the most explicit details of how and when, which categorically prohibited them from taking liberties with anything regarding the business accounts, with anyone else's affairs, with punctuality and with absences. The mere idea of getting sick was out of the question, not to mention coming to work sick (fear of contagion). She was an all-vigilant eye for absolute compliance to what was in the code. The first employees ended up leaving, but then acquired such a reputation for being bad workers that they couldn't find another job and they went far away, where their infamy hadn't reached. The other employees stayed for years, more for fear of exile than for anything else, since besides the nuisance of having to work constantly and to practice excessive courtesy, the salary wasn't incentive enough anyway and a good part of what there was went to the necessities of ties and coats, and to being clean shaven with a military cut (straight up and well scraped).

Their only son was born after five years of marriage, when gossip was already rampant that the poor woman was sterile; so thin, pale, shrunken and besides the couple probably went to bed the same distance apart as on their routine walks, in silence, from exactly six-thirty to seven-forty-five on the dot. The pregnancy wasn't obvious because she used to wear an ample housecoat, which kept those tongues of verbal journalism wagging in parlors, in markets and in formal and informal encounters, about whether she was really pregnant or if the baby was adopted. The doubt remained for a long time, as we will see later on.

In the main inventory ledger, he wrote in an accountant's calligraphy: male, seven and a half pounds, 52 centimeters long, ugly, and a crier. After two days she went back to work, a little paler and bent over a little more, wearing a proud smile, but paying no attention to the congratulations offered her, and she never even acknowledged the little presents the employees brought her. Enough already, he had said, of them sticking their noses into places they didn't belong.

He tried to become mayor by the traditional means; courting the politicians from this party and that (since one must be prudent), and throwing banquets for them and giving them modest contributions (since there were diminishing returns). And then nothing. After their victories, they couldn't recall having met him.

The flood that year from the torrential, endless rains, which didn't stop even in time to dry out the balcony that had been converted into a shimmering pool where crickets and fallen leaves splashed, brought him his long-awaited opportunity. The rising waters from the two streams, inoffensive in the summer, swept away entire neighborhoods of houses made of mud, tin, cardboard, old rags and rotten wood. Thousands were left hungry and homeless. Two old women and seven children who were sleeping in hammocks were found swollen, among the rocks, when the waters receded.

He raised the prices in his chain of businesses, but invented opportune charity. In the supermarket, long lines formed for the handout of a hard roll. In the hardware store, one could get a burlap shirt. In the bookstore the free item was the prayer, "Lord deliver us from our sins."

With a dictionary and the patience to carefully scour twenty pages a day, he found the word that described him: Philanthropist, "he who professes love for his peers and tries to improve their lot in life." He demanded that it precede his name each time someone addressed him. She was the first to call him Mister Philanthropist and at work it soon spread. The majority of their customers, not knowing the meaning of the word, believed he had changed his name, and without much difficulty they began to call him "don Philanthropist."

And the title was being reinforced with small acts: whatever was truly useless from the inventory was to be donated to the hospital, to the school, to the community center; the wilted vegetables wouldn't be sold for a few cents to don Anibal's pig farm; repackaged, they could be distributed to the poor on Saturdays at two o'clock on the dot; and, with the paper that yellowed, he decided to produce bimonthly almanacs to give to his customers, with the holidays and the lunar movements as well as blurbs of propaganda for his businesses, in which it was always mentioned that his principal concern was purely philanthropical.

The politicians visited him again, this time not to ask for a contribution, but to offer him the post of mayor. After they had nominated him the first time, reelections followed until what had to happen happened.

One of his first acts was to set aside the date of January second of each year for receiving the public from the balcony of his house high on top of the hill. He, above, would list an inventory of all he had accomplished, mixing some thoughts about moral and practical order in with the details. She, below, standing in the doorway that opened to the kitchen, would pass out corn liquor in paper cups and some homemade cookies. Then they would turn up the radio, tuned to the station that broadcast whatever music was popular, and some young and rhythmical couples would try out their moves on the pavement.

Yes, that tradition of the second of January lasted for a long time, but one day it ended.

Their son was growing and he wasn't dark like his father, nor long of face like his mother, but he was troublesome like both. He began with tantrums which neither punishment nor reward could stop. They tried beating him; it was useless. They offered him more expensive gifts, if only he would stop shouting and kicking for a while, but to no avail. They finally gave up and let him do whatever he felt like and then he began to spit at mealtime and to break valuable objects and to mock his parents in the most ridiculous ways he could. They tied him up in a dark room but he managed to escape; they would hide him when visitors arrived but he would appear at the most interesting part of the conversation to pee in the center of the rug. They didn't know what to do. He said the boy was like his mother and she, while never directly contradicting him, would answer that she couldn't recall ever behaving like that. Finally they decided that the best solution would be to send him to one of those correctional centers, to see if they could work a miracle.

They didn't see him for many years, not even during vacations, or at Christmas, or on anniversaries or birthdays. Nevertheless, in truth his absence weighed on them, as did the recurring nightmare that he would return unchanged. They sent the monthly check on time, but they never opened any correspondence that came from the institution, so they knew nothing of his progress or his setbacks. Then the day arrived that both had awaited with an intemperate fear that kept them awake at nights: the refund that the Director brought them, in person, along with a bill for five zeros preceded by a seven, because that scowling young man with the aggressive stare, a lascivious beginning of a mustache, long, curly hair, that thin, tall young man with his shoulders thrown back as if he expected a punch or were about to throw one, had burned down an entire building at the institution. He didn't smile nor say how do you do and entered like a dog with its tail between its legs. They wrote out the check and, excusing themselves without waiting to hear anything more, bid farewell to the Director. They offered him neither a seat nor a glass of water, even though the day was hot, a day with a brilliant, intruding sun that caused migraines with its harsh reflections in shoe buckles, in tooth fillings and in everything that shimmered.

From then on they never spoke with their son. He did whatever he took a fancy to, getting up much later than his parents, eating some fruit, and then on a whim that changed with the rhythm of the music, turning up the radio to its maximum volume, until the shrill tones seemed about to explode. When his parents came in, he would begin to sing, in a soft voice, the most shameless of mambos, cumbias and meringues, and then he would leave to roam the streets at all hours of the night until a fuzzy pre-dawn made ghosts of the bushes and the huts that had begun to burgeon again near the streams.

The mayor blessed the days that were calm, the mayoress made promises while she prayed novena after novena amidst the sums of the invoices, the list of orders and her responsibilities to the customers.

But the complaints began to arrive. At first they were timid. Don Anibal, rubbing his hands with the air of a diplomat beginning the process of an appeal, spoke of two dead pigs, his best pure-bred ones and already sold at a very good price, that the boy killed with arrows the night before last when the moon shone like a breast full of milk. They took care of it with a check and a plea for his silence. The list continued, ranging from a broken window to the rape in the park, right there in the corner of the lilies that were ruined worse than the poor girl, the illegitimate daughter—it was said—of Pascual the drayman and who knows for sure who her mother was but she appeared in the arms of the crippled Chepa, who shouted "She's a gift from God!"

One night, almost in the shadow of the doorway, at seven-forty-five on the dot, he walked back two steps and shouted at her: "It's over. I'm going to kill him!" She, as if expecting that and worse, answered in an unswerving voice "your will be done." They didn't go to bed, sitting instead in uncomfortable chairs in the foyer, where they used to receive those bothersome men who brought them complaints about pipes and sewers, and waited until midnight. When they were nodding off, their mouths open, the slamming of the door aroused them. "Mother, Father," said the youth, kneeling before them, "I'm going to change, I want to be a useful man, a revolutionary." They couldn't budge. They really didn't believe him; they were the kind of people that prayed for miracles without faith.

But the change did take place; the boy entered school, serious, with books under his arm that he actually read and studied, he got wonderful grades, associated with the best people, even went to the most humble ghettos where he taught the poor to read and add and subtract. Educated, sober, he spoke very little with his parents, just whatever was necessary. Of course he never followed the strict code demanded by family life, and on one memorable occasion he even said to a servant in that loud voice meant for everyone to hear: "Those pricks are two petty, compulsive, heartless imbeciles." That hurt them slightly; it wasn't enough to offend them nor to brood over. The change had been that miraculous.

He continued suspecting, she continued with her promises and novenas of gratitude, but deep down they couldn't understand the change and for a long time they rather expected a knife in the back.

The son went to the capital, to go to college. They breathed more easily, since at least they would have a long rest and perhaps luck would have it that he wouldn't find his way back home because it's pretty there, the city lights, all kinds of entertainment and girls that know how to stimulate the mind, although perhaps there wasn't much there to stimulate.

The second of January was celebrated from then on with more splendor, since they needed to replenish lost prestige and make everyone forget the many years they had been corrupting the office and tiring the public, lest anyone begin to think that a new broom might sweep better than the old one. They served beer instead of corn liquor and bologna sandwiches instead of cookies. One January second the mayor, after exaggerating the feats of his government and citing as his own some things that had been done by international organizations and volunteer associations, meditated out loud (so he said) about human ingratitude, even that of one's own children, and pointed out that philanthropy doesn't always reap gratitude. As his voice was trembling, he stirred emotion in some, especially when they saw her handing out the beers with eyes that welled up as if they were about to flood. They didn't know that the poor thing was suffering from a crippling flu that had arrived from the port in the form of an epidemic.

The son returned home, without the girl who stimulates minds. He didn't even let his parents know, nor did he visit them. He set up a law practice in a poor neighborhood and lived in the back room. A good litigator, he won hopeless cases, in eternal disputes over water rights and farm boundaries, and thus his reputation spread and people from all over, even from the capital, consulted him. He dressed cleanly and simply, and the depth of his eyes was striking. A pretty little husband-hunter noted that his look was messianic. Although few understood the term, many repeated it because it sounded nice.

When it came time for the election, he ran for mayor. That really shook up the people: father against son. Then the speeches began and what a way of speaking the boy had, clear and peremptory, concrete and sincere, especially when he talked about eradicating philanthropy so that truth and justice could thrive; and ending all these monopolies, the hardware store, the printing press, bookstore and supermarket, all with high prices and terrible products, so that people could establish honorable, free businesses; he ridiculed the compulsive little habits of that compulsive couple of the house high on top of the hill.

He won the election by such an absolute majority that according to his own count, the old mayor received votes from only himself, his wife, two servants and five of his employees. Devastated, they took a vacation to the coast, not even waiting until the inauguration. Their first vacation in 27 years of marriage and they didn't know what resting was all about nor what one could do if one didn't work. The truth was that their only wish was to go to the sea and cry and cry. Both had the idea that it was easier and more comfortable to cry by the ocean.

The young mayor arrived for his first day of work exactly on time. In his hand he was carrying his first memo: "I categorically prohibit anyone from speaking to me from behind because that always gives me a chill; anyone who shakes hands with me must first wash his hand, I'm allergic to dust and dirt; I don't want anyone to rearrange my papers and please no smoking in my presence, the odor of tobacco makes me nauseous; someone less impor-

tant should take care of small nuisances, as only the most important matters should come to my attention, those things that require
a difficult and intelligent solution; upon my entrance one should
say to me simply: good day, Mr. Mayor, on my exit: good night,
Mr. Mayor. As soon as we're better acquainted, I will give you further instructions."

And that is just how it happened. And that and other matters
which don't fit into this story, like the conditions that he expressed
very clearly and categorically to the young woman to whom he
raised the possibility of marriage, confirmed in the town that he
really was, after all, the legitimate son of the compulsive couple
of the house high on the hill.

Translated by Linda Britt

The Snow White Guard

Luisa Valenzuela

Way in the back, behind the glass, the plants are in something of an enormous case. And here in front, also in a glass case (armored) is the guard. He has something in common with the plants, a special secret that comes to him from the earth. And between one glass cage and the other, already beginning to look old, yet so tidy in their impeccable suits and their exact smiles, the young assistant managers work painstakingly. It is true that they are less dignified than the guard, but as young assistant managers of a financial firm, they are not trained to kill and that redeems them a little. Not too much. Just the little bit necessary to be able to bestow upon them the favor of imagining them—as our guard usually imagined them—making love on the carpet. In unison, oh yes, to the syncopated rhythm of the electronic calculators. Beneath them, the secretaries are also sadly pretty, almost always with light colored eyes, and the guard contemplates them, not without a certain degree of lust, and thinks that the blonde assistant managers—almost all of them also have aqueous eyes—are in a better position than he to seduce the young secretaries.

Nevertheless, he has the Parabellum, and he also has—hidden in his executive briefcase—a telescopic sight and one of the best foreign-made silencers. In an inner pocket of his jacket he carries his gun permit, the card that vouches for him as a guardian of the law. In the other pocket, heaven only knows what he has, even he doesn't usually bother to check: once he found a lipstick and smeared his hands with the red as if it were blood, another time he found unidentified seeds; on one occasion he lost his way in the fuzz of the pocket, among tobacco strands and other things, and now he doesn't even want to think about that pocket while he watches over the clients who enter and exit from the vast offices. He knows that the assistant managers may have light colored eyes, but his glass enclosure has three round eyes (one on each open side, the fourth side is up against the wall), and they are more exotic eyes, not to mention more practical and eventually more lethal. Through them one can shoot at anyone who deserves it, and from there one can feel safe and secure: that enclosure is his mother and contains him.

From his glass enclosure he sees the most absurd beings file by, some with dwarfs' faces, for example, or women whose shapes defy all rules of esthetics and little girls with hair dyed the color of egg yolk. At moments our guard thinks that the firm hires them in order to show off the physical beauty of its own employees, but he quickly discards that crazy idea: this is a financial firm, designed to make money not to spend it on absurd projects.

And him? Why is he there? He is there to protect the money, and he would water the plants too, if only they would let him.

It would do him good from time to time to be able to go over to the other glass enclosure, the one in the back; it is quite a bit larger than his although it is not armored, it is airier, and the distance from plant (*planta*) to money (*plata*) is only one letter. A distance that he would happily cross, above all because the money belongs to other people, it will never be his, and in contrast the plants don't belong to anyone. They have their own life; he could water them, cherish them, even talk to them softly as if they were a friendly dog, like that fellow who spent his days taking tender

care of his loved ones—a bulldog and a carnivorous plant. He
doesn't need to feel any attachment to the people in that office
although he is there to defend them, to risk his life for them. It's
just that nothing ever happens there: no one comes in with a
threatening look or attempts a robbery. Sometimes a suspicious
package left on a seat draws his attention, but the person who had
left it there soon comes back and goes off again, looking self-satisfied,
with the package in question under his arm. Therefore, even supposing that there had been a bomb in the package, it would explode
far from the sacrosanct offices. And his duty involves protecting
only the firm, not the entire city, much less the universe. His duty
is simply that: to act in defense, not to take the offensive, even
though if he had half a brain he would know that the potential
assailant could very well be one of their own (a man like himself,
just to mention one) and not some outsider as might be the case
with the safe. But my life is going to cost them dearly, he says to
himself often, repeating the phrase so often heard during training,
without realizing that each mortal being thinks the same thing,
with or without the law's permission (a life isn't some little thing
that one hands over just like that, much less one's own life, but
he has a license to kill and feels calm). For that reason, he sleeps
serenely at night when he isn't on guard and sometimes dreams
of the little plants in the back. That is, of course, when he isn't
lucky enough to dream about the pretty secretaries, naked, somewhat flat and one-dimensional, but always exciting. Dreams that
are more like being on guard (being awake), daydreams in which
the beautiful men and women of the financial firm tumble around
naked on the carpet which silences their movements. The carpet
as a silencer. He, there in his crystal enclosure—Snow White, damn
it—also has a pistol with a silencer, and besides he remains silent
as a plant. Almost vegetable. He is silent in his glass cage, caressing his silencer as he imagines those outside his enclosure in posi-
tions completely out of keeping with polite society.

And here he is, engrossed in his daydreams, wholeheartedly
defending that which doesn't belong to him in the very least. Not
even remotely. A perfectly imbecilic life. Defending what?: the strong

box, the honor of the secretaries, the self-confidence of the managers, assistant managers, and the rest of the employees (their tidy appearance). Defending the clients. Defending the dough that belongs to others.

The idea occurred to him one fine day, the next day he forgot it, he remembered it a week later, and then little by little the idea began to establish itself in his head permanently. A touch of humanness after all, the spark of an idea. Something was growing within him, piping hot like his affection for the plants in the back. Something called a bone of contention.

He began to go to work dragging his feet, now he didn't feel like such a big deal. He didn't dream in front of the mirror any more that his was a job for heroes.

What a revelation the day that he discovered (way inside of himself, in that part of himself whose existence he hadn't even suspected) that his purported hero's position was a jackass's job! Anybody with any balls doesn't have to use them defending others. It was if someone had given him the famous kiss on the sleeping forehead, as if someone had shaken him awake. Enlightened.

All these things were impossible for him to communicate to his bosses. Of course, he was used to keeping his mouth shut, to guarding within himself, like a treasure, those few emotions that had been blossoming in him over the course of his life. Not many emotions, scarcely the notion that something was happening in him in spite of himself. And without uttering a word, he had endured that long course, as well as the torture to his own body, called training: therefore it wasn't a question of sitting down to talk—sit down, since when in front of his superiors?—to discuss doubts or present complaints. Thus, he began little by little to nurture his overly enlightening disgruntlement, and he could spend the afternoons standing inside his glass cage focusing his thoughts on something more concrete than the erotic daydreams. He stopped imagining the young assistant managers tumbling around with the secretaries on the soft, fluffy carpet and began to see them exactly as they were, carrying out their specific duties. Coming and going in silent respect, astutely managing money, stocks, bonds, drafts, foreign currency. And all of them so offensively young, attractive.

It was good for a few months to strip those bodies of all illusions and to see them only in their purely work-related functions. Our guard became realistic, systematic. He took to coming out of the cage and strolling his flexible countenance through the rooms scattered with desks, he began to exchange a few words with the most accessible employees, he smiled at the secretaries, he chatted a long while with one of the stockbrokers. He became friends with the doorman. To some people he even mentioned his attraction to plants, and once, when he noticed that they were withered, he asked permission to water them on his own time. As they closed up the offices, they began to leave him taking care of the plants, spraying them, cleaning them with lampblack so they could breathe easy.

One afternoon he carried his passion to the extreme of staying behind two hours, serenely drinking his *maté* among the plants. The night watchman couldn't help but mention it to his superiors, and all feared that the guard might be turning into a poet, something much too dangerous in a job like his. But there was no reason to fear further deterioration: he executed his duties conscientiously and proved himself excessively alert in his hours of watch duty, not allowing any detail to escape him. He even managed to thwart a dangerous attack thanks to his fast reflexes and to a nose which won the praise of his bosses. He accepted his reward with supreme dignity, conscious of the fact that he hadn't done anything but protect his own interests. His immediate superiors as well as the directors of the firm, all present at the simple ceremony, perceived the humility of the guard as a noble sentiment, as a sincere pleasure in a duty well performed. Thus they doubled the amount of the reward and retired tranquilly to their respective homes knowing that the financial firm would be protected by unexcelled vigilance.

Thanks to the double bonus, the guard was able to equip himself as he wished and only needed to put into practice the patience learned from the plants. When he finally considered the moment appropriate, he struck with such skill that it was impossible to follow his trail and discover his whereabouts. That is to say, in the eyes of the others, he managed to realize his old dream. That is to say, he disappeared from the face of the earth (the earth swallowed him).

Translated by Sharon Magnarelli

Cage Number One

Dora Alonso

The monkey's eyes shone in the dawn light, peering in every direction. Getting up, she crept toward the bars of the cage, overcome by the desire to escape confinement. Her belly was full and she wasn't troubled by lust, but she needed contact with the leaves that had surrounded her since she first opened her wrinkled eyelids in that place.

Every night, as she crouched in her cement cubicle at the back of the cage, the last thing she saw were the trees. When she awoke, she looked for them. If there was a wind, or if it rained, the rain polished them; if the tiny leaves danced and the thunder made the buds tremble, the monkey watched, feeling herself fill up with green shoots that were born of her longing—ungraspable, tenacious...

She watched vaguely, motionless under the swaying branches that swept above the cage. Her mother, her grandmother, twenty generations of primates contemplated the leaves through her fixed gaze.

With her snout encased in a funnel of black, flexible and lukewarm skin, she held fast to the bars. Above her, the whispering of the seeds telling secrets began, the tide of rising sap in the shadow, the single words from the branches broken by the heavy dew. . . She stood still, her thin hand suspended in the air, not feeling the need to mortify her flesh with the hunter's thumb any more. Uneasiness sharpened her teeth, pressed on her temples. She screeched in fright and curled herself up with her arms behind her head, to protect herself from some fear that lurked nearby, in the moist dawn grass.

Terror made her crouch next to the concrete, an eternal wall. The same words, the same voice, the song, the lisp, spoke to her always, calling her. Every muscle in her body wanted to respond at once. She jumped, but as she did she whimpered indecisively. She babbled on, shaken by a restlessness that was killing her.

Approaching the bars for a second time, she held on with both hands and showed her black face, long and sorrowful as a death mask. The iron felt cold and hostile. Its smoothness penetrated the tips of her fingers and she encircled the bars with her whole hand, squeezing hard. Surging with fury, she shook the bars. The iron began to yield and bend. The monkey walked through.

Now that she was calmer, the snores from Pipa's cubs and the trailing of a lizard through the dry brush did not disturb her.

From his circular cage, the gibbon cried, hanging his lament from the expectant trees, on long faded branches.

The monkey passed like a shadow through the stillness of the sleeping park.

The great prison breathed in the night, liberating its vegetable dreams, the tortured nightmares of free rivers and rapid deaths, the fever of sterile encounters, the castrated anger of confinement.

She trotted aimlessly, touching the earth with the knuckles of her closed hands, her head low. What was born that night kept shaking her with the cooing of the wind, with the breath, the complaint, the secret.

She stopped at the tree: it was weeping leaves and sighs. The monkey's eyes filled up like two wells of happiness. The mantle spilled over, pouring silk and freshness from above. Everything scorching her inside was extinguished. Oh, oh, oh, the chatter of monkeys drenched her with happiness. Oh, oh. She climbed up the trunk and its roughness penetrated her, bleeding her of unknown flowers. Embracing the tree, she tried to grasp it and drink what was coursing beneath the bark.

She touched a branch with her forehead and the wet leaves brushed lips that were desperately pressed together. She moaned and moaned, closing her eyes languid with fever. The bowls of water and fruit, the swing and the hoop were very far away on this first free morning.

The monkey was delirious, dreaming she was biting the good keeper on the throat until she could feel her lips near his flowing arteries; she strangled him with the shoelaces that he had taught her to tie and untie. She dreamed she was fleeing to the forest followed by all the simians deformed in exhibitions:

Orangutans from the dense jungles of Sumatra and Borneo, red like living flames, the "savage men" of the far-off island.

Gibbons from the islands of Indonesia, the beloved Unka-Pati of Malaysia with long arms, agile as arrows.

Patriarchal gorillas from the plains and from the mountains, skilled at climbing and hanging from branches; like sailors, masters of a hundred knots. Two hundred kilos of defeated bulk and several meters wide when they stretched out their arms.

Chimpanzees of inconceivable force, impetuous, of the highest intelligence; white-faced, black-faced, bald, pygmies, flying through the branches when they heard the tom-tom of the leader of the herd on the hollow trunks, ordering the beginning of the war dance.

The monkey felt them close behind her, in an unending multitude...

Baboons with gaudy reddish callouses; short-tailed, omnivorous mandrills, their beastly bluish masks striped with colors, the untiring trot. Papions sacred to India, warlike, shrewd, stone-throwers. Their rival baboons. Amadrias with thick shoulder capes, worshipped by the ancient Egyptians.

Grotesque rhinotipecs with brilliant blue skin an large turned-up noses, from the eternal snows of Tibet; petty thieves, crazed by the flasks...

Angry green monkeys.

Frantic macaques, swimmers and collectors of algae and crabs, native to Japan, the Philippines, China, Java, with long tails and pink faces.

There were a thousand noises: wails, trills, chirps, barks, whistles, grunts.

They descended in waves from the Old World, joining monkeys of America with prehensile tails. From the Sierra Madre to Paraguay, the members of the great desolate family came from the young continent.

Beautiful black and copper-colored howlers, inhabitants of the torrential jungles of the Amazon basin.

Capuchins, curious and blinking like little old people.

Spider monkeys, like mute dummies.

Pacific fat-bellies.

Micos from Peru, from Matto Grosso, eaters of grasshoppers and scorpions.

Multicolored herds of silky titis: titi-lion cub, its mane of fluffy virgin gold, golden yellow: white feathery titis from barren Catinga; squirrel titis and ones with paintbrush hair...

Coveted pygmy monkeys from Ecuador, weighing eighty grams (jewel and ambition of courtesans), with newborn hands that a magnifying glass can barely uncover.

The colored dwarves came leaping over the vast green heights. Their long caravan was joined by the monkeys enslaved in circuses and by street musicians.

The diseased, blind monkeys ran stumbling, saved from the distant aristocratic properties of Havana, when their forgetful owners, fleeing from the armed populace, left the country, condemning them to death by starvation.

There came others, degenerated by captivity: those who had destroyed each other with their teeth in the rampant fire, finding no escape for their inhibited desire. The sadistic and murderous Martin Perez. And the pleasure-hungry cripple forced by the law of demand to satisfy himself with any living thing that moved nearby: pigeon, man, tiger or frog.

At the front line, with tooth and nail, the great Toto, the trusty chimpanzee who threw excrement, spat at the curious, at children, old people, soldiers or women whom he attacked with his imprisoned sex.

The delirious fugitive penetrated the fragrant green foliage curtain, possessing it for all those of her species who suffered imprisonment, with her nerves, her brain and her eyes covered and laced with roots, leaves and invisible, untouched branches.

The hairy hands with the opposing thumb grasped the branches. They broke one, hanging it at the crown of the tree to start a nest.

As she snapped the branch in two and wove it into place, the sun came out.

*   *   *

Along the avenue where the flamboyan trees opened their red umbrellas, a keeper was arriving. He stopped in front of cage number one, looked inside and shouted to send the word to the dwarf:

"Look, Simon: the monkey's dead!"

Translated by Miriam Ben-Ur and
Lorraine Elena Roses

A Child, A Dog, The Night

Jimena's Fair

Laura Riesco

"You can sit here for a while before it gets cold, but don't go playing in the dirt and don't even think about opening that gate," Old Nanny says to her, drying her veined and red hands in her apron and returning hurriedly to her tasks in the kitchen. Jimena sits on the top step (there are five steps going up to the back door of the house) and arranges her dress beneath her legs because in spite of it being a June afternoon, the cement is still cold. Several yards from her is the white painted fence and to the right in the fence is the section that opens and closes with an old-fashioned iron latch. If she bounces on one of the horizontal boards that go across the bottom of the fence, Jimena can make the latch fly up and suddenly the gate is freed and she swings for a minute hanging on to the latch until the rusty hinges stop squeaking. People they know well who come frequently to the house and enter by the kitchen door stick a hand in through the vertical planks and lift up the latch to get in. Don Sebastian's son, the one who delivers firewood, and he's not very tall—he's only a few years older than she—climbs up anywhere along the fence with no problem and jumps down on the other side with a self-satisfied smile. Then Jimena smiles at him accepting his feat as she would a gift, but she is disheartened whenever this happens because it makes her realize a little more that the fence and the latch do not protect the family from outsiders so much as they keep her barricaded in this dry piece of land they call the back yard, for want of a better word. It cannot be called a garden because the dust and the altitude do not allow grass or flowers to grow there, and it is not a barnyard because they have no animals.

From the step Jimena looks, with a habit that has acquired the fervor of a ritual, out past the fence. Beyond the empty field, wide and sterile, with no trees, not even any green weeds, sometimes she can see the train that goes by twice a day and that disappears very fast, too fast, to the right or to the left. The rhythmic rattling of the train is usually the last sound she hears before she falls asleep at night. She listens to it, making it keep time with any melody she remembers from the radio; she lets herself go, go far away with the song and the rhythm until she cannot hear it any more, and the melody loses its enchantment, the silence brings her back to her pillow, to the walls of her room. Beyond the tracks (that she can't see but imagines) she can hardly distinguish the shapes in the camp where the workers from the foundry live; she has a confused idea of the camp because she has passed by it only a few times and then in a car. She closes her eyes and fixes her attention on the place as if it were a blurred photograph that lost, over time, the clarity of the objects photographed. She sees a large gray mass, monotony stretching out in endless small doors and windows all the same, dark spaces, holes where nothing, not even air, seemed to move, to enter or leave. Nonetheless, there are people there, a lot of people, Old Nanny told her grumbling, so many that the company will have to build another camp some day. Jimena has stopped asking questions about the immobile stripe in the distance because the answers are evasive and she senses that it makes the adults feel uncomfortable. Her mother, especially, sighs and becomes a bit sad. When Jimena watches beyond the fence for a long time, when the train reminds her of that other side and bewildering questions rise in her throat, she holds herself back and asks them to tell her stories or she goes, obediently, to look at the color pictures in her father's encyclopedia or the picture album in her mother's bedroom.

Today, in any case, lost in thought, she contemplates the reflection of the sun, hardly sun at all, hardly lukewarm on the corrugated roofs. Then she sees an orange or bright pink color that rises in the distance, rises from the very earth on the horizon and erases the hazy picture memory evokes. She breathes deeply, closes her eyelids hard and then opens them to see if the colors are really still there in the distance or if they are like the other ones she manages to see (although she knows they are not there) on the walls of her room when she is bored and cannot sleep. Trembling, she watches a city of arches, cupolas, high towers, bright, shining castles and more than anything balloons, hundreds of balloons being let go by an invisible hand and rising up, merry and singing, from this city in celebration, waving and made all of oranges. She runs to the kitchen door and yells for Old Nanny to come out and look.

"Come here, Nanny!" she pulls her, tugging on her skirt. "Come and see how pretty the camp is, they're having a fair!"

The Old Nanny cannot go out as quickly as she would like to because age has made her move slowly and drag her feet, but, complaining, she takes Jimena's hand and goes out with her to look.

"There's nothing there," she says angrily, pulling her back toward the house. "And it's cold. Go on inside."

Over her shoulder, almost in tears, insisting on the existence of what she has seen, she manages to see the empty field over the tops of the fence posts and beyond, instead of the fair, she now sees nothing either.

*   *   *

Several days ago they brought the Young Nanny from the ranch in the valley. Her mother, one night, after praying with her the Our Father and the Hail Mary, tells her she is going to have a new nanny.

"But I've got a nanny, I've had her for years!"

"That's why," she tells her, covering her with her blankets. "Because it's been so long and now she's very old and she gets tired. Besides, she can't see well. Haven't you noticed?"

She speaks in a whisper as if Old Nanny, who at this time of night is in her room at the other end of the house, could hear her. It is true that she no longer sees very well. She has very fine spider webs over her eyes, and they used to be black but are changing to gray. It is also true that she gets tired, that she walks with difficulty and painfully when she has to move quickly and that she has gotten to be more of a scold than ever.

"But she won't return to the valley, will she?"

She struggles not to let her voice tremble. She has heard her mother on occasion affectionately suggest that she return to the ranch. We don't want you to go Mama Christina, but here you do too much and there you'll have more peace and quiet, she proposes. She has to raise her voice so that Old Nanny can hear her because she is also getting a little deaf. Even speaking loudly her mother's voice bears the affection and respect she has always felt for the old woman.

"If I leave, child," she always answers, "your house will be topsy-turvy. You still can't handle it, you don't know how."

Her mother does not insist. They keep on talking, telling each other things, making decisions, arrangements. Old Nanny must have been very tired to have agreed to let another servant come. In the past she has become impossible whenever they have brought a girl from the valley to help her, so impossible that after a few days they send the girl back to the ranch. Her father complains, we know who's the boss in this house, he says, but her mother argues that she likes to do housework and that it won't hurt them to save a little money. This time, however, Old Nanny has not protested the arrival of her helper. One morning Jimena wakes up and sees beside her mother a young girl dressed in a black skirt, a shawl knotted on her chest. She tries not to stare at the girl's thick bare feet, at her black, hardened toenails. The girl smiles with unabashed curiosity. Jimena vaguely remembers having played with her at the ranch.

"Jimena," says her mother, "Maria Ester is going to be your new nanny."

Since the other one has always been the Old Nanny, Maria Ester enters into her mind first, and later, at times, in the speech of the others, too, as the Young Nanny.

At first she gives her a hard time on purpose. She pretends not to understand her clumsy Spanish that comes out in a knotty voice and she makes fun of her by imitating her. She purposely mixes up the routine of daily household chores that the girl learns with such difficulty, not because she is slow-witted but because there is so much to learn. She doesn't obey her, and to make her rejection clear she runs more frequently than ever to seek refuge in Old Nanny's lap, who, after she hugs her, sets her aside, scolding her in a low voice: "You should be ashamed of yourself! Behaving like this when, well, what has she done to you?"

The Young Nanny does not take it to heart. She is pretty and laughs a lot and sings while she works. Jimena has been accepting her little by little because she is enchanted by her stories of her village in the valley. It does not take Maria Ester long to figure out Jimena's soft spot and she gains the upper hand, she gets her on her side, buys her good behavior with fantastic tales that weave together planting and harvest time, the festivities of Carnaval and Christmas, the magic of certain plants, of certain hands that can kill or cure, suffering souls that search endlessly for peace or for vengeance, the miracles of dark-skinned saints who carry a staff or silver rings when they rise proud over the sacred mountains. Some of these things she has already heard from Old Nanny, but in the Young Nanny they appear from far away, flutter pathetically, seem to want to disappear as soon as they are conjured up. The Young Nanny tells stories from the heart, with noises, leaps, horrible faces. Jimena is terrified but she always wants more. She follows the Young Nanny around the house, holding the yellow rag she uses to help her dust the furniture, urging her, "And? And then?" The Young Nanny says with a teasing tilt of the head that makes her thick black braids fall to one side, "I'll tell you later."

The stories are full of the pleasure and the temptation of what is forbidden because both her mother and Old Nanny have asked her not to let her talk in Quechua until she knows the new language well.

"But she talks in Spanish!" she argues, whimpering.

"No, Jimena, you don't realize it. She starts in Spanish and ends up in Quechua. Besides, you walk around scared all the time, as if you were seeing ghosts on the walls. You jump at any little thing and you always seem ready to fly off."

It is true that she goes around sometimes with her heart in her throat and that sometimes she speaks in Quechua and she understands almost everything. Her mother and Old Nanny mix the two languages, too, because of habit or sometimes when they don't want her father to understand. If Jimena cannot figure out how to translate a word from a story, she goes running to Old Nanny to ask her what it means. The old woman at first answers her, without paying much attention, but after a few days comes to scold the girl, who, both shy and smiling, bites her lips mumbling OK, you don't have to yell, it's alright.

Jimena has learned not to ask anymore. Sometimes if it rains the night before, the two of them go out in the yard to make dishes for her dolls from the wet earth. Squatting down she listens to her, enthralled, and it no longer bothers her to think that by the next day the tiny pots that they have made with such care, irritating the skin of their hands, will look ugly and misshapen and will break at the slightest movement. Because Jimena is at a loss for what to say to her, one morning she waves her hand, on which the cold air has dried the clay, toward the empty field.

"One afternoon," she says confidentially, "I saw a very pretty fair, all orange with lots of balloons way over there by the camp."

Young Nanny turns her head to the right and squints to look.

"Oh, really?" she answers, not convinced.

This disagreement annoys Jimena and she smashes the little flower vase that Young Nanny is rolling between her fingers. She runs to the house leaving behind her pieces of clay that immediately dry up as they fall in the doorway.

*   *   *

Her mother is making arrangements for them to go down to the ranch in a few days. Jimena watches her bustling and fluttering about the house, bumping into things, as if she did not know where the furniture was placed, or where the walls began and ended. Now and then she sighs deeply and lets her head fall to one side with that gesture that seems so mournful to Jimena. In the midst of preparations to go to the valley, that tend to be exhausting but cheerful, Jimena suspects that something is wrong.

"Is Grandpa sick?" she asks as her mother fixes her hair.

"No," she answers as she fastens the barrette. Irritated, she reprimands her. "Where do you get these ideas from?" That's all we need. Thank God that there everything is alright."

Jimena would like to ask then what is it that is wrong here, but her mother's tone frightens off her words. She notices that sometimes the telephone rings very late, too late, even when her father is already asleep. From her bed she hears him go to the dining room to answer it and she wants to hear, find out what is happening even though she is afraid, but he talks very quietly, mumbling between his teeth, or even, hesitatingly in English. She has seen her mother, also near the telephone, pass a perfumed handkerchief over her eyes and she has heard her say she is very, very troubled by the situation. In the last few days Jimena has noticed the absence of their usual visitors. Her mother's friends, the Peruvians and the Americans, don't get together like before to have tea. Only Mr. Estevez comes to visit, not as often as before, always when it is beginning to get dark, leaning on his silver-handled cane, dragging his wooden leg and making smoke rings for her when he catches her looking at him. They talk in the dining room as they drink coffee and sit for along time after dinner. They do not let her bring her dolls and play at the foot of the table like they used to.

"Maria Ester," her mother calls, "take Jimena into the kitchen to play."

She could make a fuss, kick a bit, start crying, but her mother's wounded air and the unspeaking eyes of Mr. Estevez, without his usual friendly wink, confuse her. They close the door that leads to the kitchen and she can hear nothing except when her father raises his voice and shouts that he's had enough and they can all go to hell.

The telephone does continue ringing constantly. It is something new, like the fact that Miss Murphy's kindergarten has closed. She misses the mornings in the widow's living room full of toys and colorful books. They cut out shapes to paste onto large pieces of cardboard and Jimena breathes in, when no one is looking, the smell of the white paste they use. She also likes the smell of the fat wax crayons and of the jam the teacher spreads on soda crackers to give them at ten o'clock. She plays with Debbie and Diana, who protect her from the more mischievous children not just because she is the smallest, but because she is just now beginning to understand a little English. She cannot explain it, and she does not want to ask why, but when she tries to find a word in English, the Quechua word comes effortlessly to her instead. Debbie and Diana live a few houses down the road and before they would come to spend the afternoon with Jimena or she would go play at their house, but she hasn't seen them now for days. It is as if the American families had all suddenly vanished into thin air.

A short while ago Don Sebastian came to drop off the firewood. He parked his truck near the fence as usual. He threw the logs they use in the fireplace any which way behind the fence. Jimena goes out when she hears the noise the wood makes as they bounce off one another. No one has seen her slip out the door and as she approaches the fence she thinks of the rides Don Sebastian always gives her in the little cart he uses to move the wood and then pile it symmetrically against the wall of the house beneath the eaves. They are crazy rides and Don Sebastian's son gets in the cart with her, too, or else he pushes the cart himself, making her think he is going to tip it over, that he is going to make her fall out and then he straightens out the cart with a skillful movement and they both laugh and laugh. This time the boy has stayed behind the fence with his hands in his pockets looking fixedly at his shoes or only in his father's direction. Jimena asks him to come in and play. The boy does not move a muscle, does not change position, just stands there as if he had not heard her. Don Sebastian barely answers her greeting with a nod of his head. The two go off unsmiling leaving the disorderly pile of wood next to the fence so that later she and Young Nanny carry it piece by piece and arrange it under the eaves. Jimena asks Old Nanny why the two are behaving like that and she answers in a bad mood that maybe they aren't feeling well. Jimena lifts the white curtain with yellow dots at the pantry window and looks at the gray sky that almost always is the same gray color. The foundry pours out a gray smoke that hangs over the town all year long like an awning. People get sick because the air carries miniscule particles that you cannot see but that make you cough and make your eyes tear. Jimena's too, although she is lucky, they have told her so many times so that she will learn to be grateful, they can whisk her by car down to the valley whenever her breathing becomes a problem.

Her favorite outings, to the town square and to the market area, have also stopped. For days Young Nanny has gone alone to do the shopping. Jimena shouted so much from the closet where they locked her in for answering back, that when she thinks of it, her throat still hurts and her chest feels heavy. She listened outside the bathroom door as her mother took her side, insisted that that was why they had brought Maria Ester from the ranch, because she is young and strong, but her father, unyielding, said better safe than sorry. From the parlor window on one side of the front door, Jimena looks at the forbidden road, the steps that she has never been allowed to sit on by herself because across the road is the rail fence she could easily pass through; beyond the rail fence is the cliff and below, the Mantaro. When Old Nanny's knees did not hurt and she used to do the marketing, she would take her to the square the other way so she would not see the river. They would go out through the patio door and would walk through the empty field staying very close to the neighbor's houses, company houses, each one identical to hers, with fences and some with swings brought from outside the country. With Young Nanny it was different, with her they went out on the river side and despite strict orders from her mother, they got close to the iron rail fence so they could look down.

"How ugly!" Young Nanny said the first time.

Jimena thinks it is beautiful. The current moves the water rapidly, and even when they arrive at the bridge, the river keeps stretching out to the right and to the left and gets lost in the distance, where she can no longer see it. The sound of the water, its continual flowing, its remote confines, make her think of the train. Jimena is used to its smell, but Young Nanny says it smells bad, she holds her nose and points with her finger to the yellow grease that forms islands that dissolve only to reappear farther away. In the valley, she says, the river is clean and you can get close to the tiny little silver fish that know how to hide under the mossy rocks. They drink its water, they wash their hair in it with a gummy substance from colorful little frogs, the girls from the valley play as they wash clothes there, they get soaking wet just like at Carnaval time. The blue sky of the valley jars her memory and then she interrupts to tell her it's a lie, it's just a story. Jimena doesn't know why, but she feels she must defend this river that she hears trembling down below those rare times when they have the windows open in the house.

*　　*　　*

They have postponed for the second time the trip to the valley. Her mother has opened the door to the storeroom where they have put the telephone, perhaps so she won't bother them while they are talking. Her face is very pale. She sits at the dining room table and she barely has the strength to call Old Nanny. Jimena runs to get her from the yard where she is hanging out the laundry with Young Nanny and the old woman comes mumbling a Hail Mary under her breath. They find her mother with her head between her arms leaning on the woven tablecloth sobbing uncontrollably. Old Nanny orders the girl to bring a glass of water and her mother hugs her waist while the old woman affectionately pats her hair. She comforts her in Quechua, but Jimena tries not to understand, she concentrates on the design the crocheted roses have imprinted on the inside of her mother's arm. When she cannot stand it any longer she goes to the bathroom and locks herself in until the weakness in her legs and the embarrassment or shyness that burns her cheeks and whistles in her chest, goes away.

A while later, as she is having a snack in the kitchen, in the midst of the silence in which she can hear herself chewing despite her efforts to avoid it, she looks closely at Old Nanny. She has gotten even older this afternoon. Jimena looks, as if it were the first time she has even noticed her, at her thin, gray braids, at her blue sweater, at her almost purple neck, full of loose folds, at her high, soft cheekbones that descend to the bags of her cheeks, those cheeks that were almost tight and that now inflate and deflate with her breathing. She does not want to see her like this. She also wants to take refuge near her apron, her tenuous yet still perceptible smell of the valley, of forest, of eucalyptus. But she is held back by the large tears she sees for the first time on her face and that are falling as if from those clouds that are covering her eyes and leaving her blind.

*   *   *

She is awake although she pretended not to be a few minutes ago when her mother came into her room to cover her. She was awakened by some blasting that could be heard from the other side of the bridge. For the last few nights her mother has come into her room frequently to check on her as if she were sick. Then she goes back to bed on tiptoe and because now they leave open the bathroom doors that join the two bedrooms, Jimena hears bits of their conversation. She hears *Lima, reinforcements, threats, fire, camp, the ranch, highway, I don't want to leave you, you must, horrifying, even with children.* She does not want to hear any more. She covers her head with the blankets, she blocks her ears with her fingers. For days the train has been off schedule, she has almost forgotten to wait for it so that its rhythm can rock her to sleep. She is no longer able to make the little shapes appear on the walls like when she plays in the dark with her eyes because she would have to take her head out from under the covers and look out.

She tries to remember the pictures in the album, one by one in the order they appear on the black pages. She brings back certain places, certain people of the valley, she and Old Nanny in different rooms of this house, friends of hers and of her parents that she recognizes in spite of changes over time, happy family occasions or company get-togethers. Most of all she is consoled by the smiles of before, her father's eyes that in photographs rarely look at the camera, but rather focus serenely on her mother. Tonight these images are painful and so, absorbing the warmth of her body, she tries to sleep and think about the orange-colored fair beyond the empty field.

*   *   *

During the morning she behaves very badly with Young Nanny. She does not want to hear her stories. She does not want to look at the pictures in the encyclopedia with her. She does not want to help her dust the furniture. She does not want to think she prefers her to Old Nanny. Maria Ester, who now insists on being called only by that name, receives these affronts without a word. She no longer laughs at everything and she quietly sings nostalgic tunes in a voice so soft that it barely reaches two chairs away. As she is drying the juice that has spilled on her dress, however, she says with a barely contained rancor, "Just so you know. They're stealing the bosses' children."

Jimena is startled without letting it be seen. She moves away giving her a push and yells to her from Old Nanny's lap, "Liar! They're just stories, just your stories."

*   *   *

Her mother has had to go out to make some last-minute arrangements for the trip. Jimena is bored and she is overwhelmed by the disorder caused by the boxes, the packages, the wrapping materials for moving. They will go to the ranch and then to Lima. Maria Ester is standing on a chair taking out the clothes, the hangers, the hats, the artificial flowers, the letters tied with blue ribbon and that have a light scent of gardenia, everything from her parents' closet. Old Nanny does not have the strength to carry things, but she is the one who decides where things go. Jimena wants to snoop around and help at the same time although she does not insist; the two women are very grumpy and they pay no attention to her, in fact they treat her like a bothersome mosquito. They tell her to go into the kitchen and eat some bread and honey. They have rolled up the rugs and the lines of the wood floor remind her of the railroad tracks. Maybe it is time for the train to go by. At any rate she prefers not to ask because she thinks they will snap at her again. She opens the curtains with the yellow dots to see outside and gets impatient because the angle is not right to see where she wants. She carefully closes the door into the dining room and opens the service door, the one that faces the empty field.

It has been a long time since they have allowed her to sit on the steps and now they are so busy they won't notice her absence. She arranges her dress under her legs so the cold from the cement does not come through. The silence is almost complete, she hears only a metallic noise like the warning signals at the railroad crossing beside the bridge. At first she thinks it is her own desire that makes her see, far over there, farther than the imagined railroad tracks, the fair, the orange city that rises up before her eyes. She turns her head to be sure no one has seen her and she heads toward the fence. From there she cannot see as well as from the top stair, but the castle towers, the myriad balloons let loose are rising through the air. For a moment she wonders if she should tell her nannies and prove to them that she was not lying, but the memory of the first experience, of how the fair disappeared when she wanted a witness, makes her change her mind. Besides there is a hot smell in the air, like from the fireplace on winter nights, and this smell hypnotizes her, makes her forget completely the possibility of calling them to see if they can see it too. She goes toward the gate, she climbs up until she reaches the latch and opens it, being careful not to make a sound. She keeps swinging, counting the loud squeaks of the hinges that could give her away. Before she gets down completely, with the toe of her patent leather shoe in the dirt, she looks around again to see if they are coming. She cannot hear anything from the house and it is not hard for her to half close the gate a take a few steps forward into the empty field. The farther she goes from the fence the hotter it becomes and the colors are so strong that they hurt her eyes, like in the valley when she tries to look straight at the sun and cannot do it. At first she is afraid they will call her, that they will pull her inside the white fence. Then, unafraid, feverish with balloons and flowers, dizzy from space, from anticipation, from the orange color that now sometimes has blue tints, she runs toward the fair without turning around even once to look back.

Translated by Janet Gold

A Child, a Dog, the Night

Amalia Rendic

The sun faded shortly in golden rays. The faint light of the street-lamps could scarcely hold back the darkness and fog that invaded the entire mining camp. A large group of men handling the pile drivers, machinists, ore workers, and miners were going home. The return journey was slow and silent because of the breathing diffi-culty caused by the thin air. The Chuquicamata mine is situated at over two thousand eight hundred meters above sea level.

As the group arrived at the Binkeroft neighborhood, it began to disperse toward different streets of the workers camp. House-hold lights could be seen through half-open windows and doors. The worker, Juan Labra, a strong machinist and loyal friend, con-tinued walking on one of the many narrow streets, still sighing because of the shrill whistles and sirens of the work areas. The wrinkles quickly vanished from his young face, which was already furrowed with deep wrinkles like veins of ore, and a burst of tender-ness filled his eyes. He readily accepted his young family's loving welcome. Little Juan was waiting at the door of the house as he did every afternoon. He was a small nine-year-old boy, with lively, curious eyes, quite strong for his age and with feet that loved to walk. For him, the mine had no secrets. He knew every inch of the mine and all of its mysteries. He was a talkative child whose constant chatter could be interrupted only by smiles. With his face pressed against the iron garden gate, he curiously watched a very tall North American who was walking behind his father.

"Dad, a gringo is following you, he is coming to our house!" he whispered, frightened, to his father. The street was deserted. Little Juan was intrigued by the presence of Black, the huge shepherd dog that followed Mr. Davies, his master. Black was one of the few beings that had managed to enter Davies' affections. A solitary companion in his lonely existence in a foreign land.

"Please come in, Mr. Davies. What can we do for you?" said the miner Juan Labra, respectfully taking off his metal hat and opening the small door of the gate. He could barely hide his astonishment at seeing one of the company's owners at his door.

"I'll be brief, Mr. Labra. I need a big favor from you. I soon must leave for Antofagasta and want to leave in your custody for a few days my good friend, Black. You'll be kind. In Calama you organized a society for the protection of animals. Everybody knows this," said Mr. Davies, looking at his dog.

"That's fine, Mr. Davies, thank you for your trust. He will be happy here. We will make sure the dog doesn't suffer. My son, Little Juan, will take care of him in my absence," promised Labra, adjusting his jacket and feeling strangely satisfied inside.

"I leave him in your hands and thank you very much. See you later, Mr. Labra. I'll return very soon, Black . . . Ah, I forgot! Here I'll leave his provisions of canned meat. It is his favorite food."

The master and his dog seemed sad. Black tugged at his master's pants, Davies bent over to pet the dog's head, with its pointed snout, and left. The animal started to follow, but Little Juan's arms held him back like chains. Black barked falteringly, sniffing the air. His red, wet tongue was hanging out of his mouth. He panted anxiously. The boy closed the gate. Black stood erect, looking lonesome. His shining fur, his slenderness, his dignified bearing, were indications of his pedigree. He was an expensive dog and had won many dog shows because of his pedigree.

The boy began talking to the dog as if it were a younger brother. For a long time they watched each other without even blinking. The dog's gaze was steady, and the boy's face was reflected in his eyes like tiny bright points. He shyly petted the back of the dog, who was sniffing the air and later responded with a reluctant movement of his tail.

Little Juan continued his strange monologue with Black. They started to become fond of each other. Across the dark, foggy hours of the night the dawn arrived. Then the day broke, as always, in the middle of the two huge mounds that formed the San Pedro and San Pablo volcanoes. Everything seemed to be a wet blue color.

Black awoke with the first sirens on the patio of the workers' house and watched the procession of miners; it was almost as if a great thing had awakened in his heart, too. He responded to these new impressions with barks that sounded like explosions. First thing in the morning, Little Juan, in a fantasy world, went out to see his new friend, and during the next few days they went everywhere together.

Challenging the wind, they ran along the winding ribbon that was the road to Calama. They tirelessly penetrated the immense vastness of the thin air.

They played together, diving into the grey residues of the copper mine pit, that shapeless, majestic mass of metallic land. They tried to collect the shining blue-green and yellow reflections that make bright colors in the sunlight.

They passed the hours this way until the nights came, the ties of the friendship that bound Little Juan and Black becoming stronger and stronger. A growing anxiety clouded the boy's short-lived happiness. He was dreading the day that their time together would end. It was certain that Mr. Davies would return.

"Papa, can't you ask the mister to give us Black? Why can't you buy him?"

"No, Little Juan, he will never be ours. He is very elegant, and worth his weight in gold. He is a rich man's dog. The gringos like to take walks with dogs like this one and present them in shows," answered the worker with a bitter smile.

"When I grow up I will buy him," responded little Juan decisively. "I don't want them to take him away! He's my friend!" he shouted at his father.

One day, as they returned from their walk on the banks of the Loa River, a nasty mountain wind began to blow. They were wet from the silky mist of Camanchaca. When they came to the door, they stopped as if in fear and dread.

"Mr. Davies!" He had returned. The little boy tried to explain what the dog meant to him, but the words welled up in his heart and stayed in his parched throat. It was a sad moment.

"Goodbye, little friend, and good luck," he stammered, weeping and wringing his hands nervously.

Mr. Davies thanked him sincerely. Like a little gentleman, the child refused to accept any payment.

Black reluctantly started to walk behind his former owner, and eagerly examining the corners of the road, said goodbye to the workers' neighborhoods on the road toward the American camp. Now that Little Juan's first encounter with despair was over, he pondered the fact that he could never have an elegant dog. Black continued his walk. The harmony settled in both of them.

But the loneliness of night came, when souls contemplate themselves to the last fragment of life itself and then everything was useless. Little Juan's defenses collapsed and he began to cry. Something provoked a flow of communication between the boy and the animal across the space and at that very moment, the dog began to howl in the American camp. Memories of Black were flashing through the boy's mind, and as if driven by a secret force, the dog barked furiously, asking the wind to transmit his message. It began as a plaintive concert, and then it became deafening.

Little Juan cried the whole night in a beseeching moan that became a strange concert that whipped through the still streets of the mining town.

Mr. Davies was bewildered by Black's behavior. What could a man do when faced with a crying dog? A new truth took possession of the gringo's mind. Black didn't belong to him anymore;

he had lost his love.

Labra could not comfort his tearful and feverish little boy. For what could a man do when faced with a crying child? Labra wanted to see his son's quick, confident smile once again. He felt obliged to win back Little Juan's smile. Poverty had stung him many times, but he could not stand this. Something extraordinary would have to happen in the mining town on this uneasy night.

As if the time had come for all men to be brothers, Labra threw his poncho on his shoulders, took the flashlight, and set off for the high neighborhood to see if a miracle could become reality. Yes, he must be courageous and daring. He, a simple laborer, always shy and silent, would ask for the elegant, beautiful, prize-winning Black from one of the company bosses. He inhaled the cold night air deeply and shuddered to think of his own boldness. He climbed up toward the American camp.

Suddenly, a pair of brown, phosphorescent eyes were glowing in the light of the lantern. Labra was startled. The smell of a pipe and fine tobacco, and a familiar bark stopped him...

Mr. Davies had gone out to see him at that very moment and had been coming toward the workers' housing area!

Something touched the hearts of the two men. Words were not necessary.

"He doesn't belong to me anymore," stammered Mr. Davies, depositing Black's heavy metal leash in the worker's hands.

Labra took the animal in his trembling hands and a melancholy happiness warmed his smile. There were no elaborate thanks, only a silent and reciprocal understanding. Black, tugging, forced him to continue following his tracks toward Little Juan's neighborhood.

In that miraculous moment, a new warmth tempered the night of Chuqui.

Translated by Miriam Ben-Ur

The Enchanted Raisin

Jacqueline Balcells

Once upon a time, there was a mom who had three, absolutely unbearable children. They did every bad and stupid thing imaginable, as well as the unimaginable ones. Several times they almost burned down the house, and they flooded it a hundred times. They broke the furniture, smashed the plates, fought and screamed like crazy people, spilled ink on the white sheets, and swung from the curtains as if they were monkeys in the jungle. And why bother saying what happened when they were sent outside: they spread panic throughout the neighborhood.

Their dad was almost never home, and their poor mother couldn't manage these three little devils. She was completely exhausted at the end of the day from chasing after them.

"My children," she said to them, "please stop your foolishness, if only this once. Look at me: each one of your pranks and screams is a wrinkle on my face. I am becoming an old lady."

And it was true. This woman, who had been tall and beautiful, was wrinkling and shrinking from one day to the next.

Her children didn't notice anything. But one day, when she went to meet them after school, their friends asked with astonishment, "Why does your grandmother come to get you now?"

The children felt bad for a moment; they were upset that their mother was mistaken for their grandmother. But they didn't think about it for long—they had so much to do!

The poor woman continued to wrinkle and shrink at an incredible rate. The moment arrived when she could no longer walk: her legs had become two little sticks that were so skinny, they were like cherry stems, and her back was so curved, she could barely see in front of her. Nevertheless, her three children did not stop inventing more and more horrible pranks:

"Let's take the feathers out of the pillows!"

"Let's pull out the dog's fur!"

"Let's cut off the cat's ears!"

"Let's dig a hole in the field for the gardner to fall into!"

By now, their mother was so small that, standing, she did not reach her youngest child's knees. She sighed, "Children, enough! Look at my size, my wrinkles. If this continues, I will shrink so much that you won't even be able to see me." But she never thought this would happen.

One night after supper, she dragged herself to her room, exhausted. She put on her nightgown, which was now one hundred times too big. She climbed on her bed, rolled herself into a ball and fell deeply asleep.

The next morning when they woke up, the children did what they always did. They jumped on their beds like devils and began to yell, "Moooooommm, bring us our breakfast!"

There was no response. They yelled louder, with no success. They began to howl, once, twice, ten times, thirty times. After the fifty-first shout, with their throats sore, they decided to go to their mother's room.

Her bed was unmade, but she was nowhere to be found. The children realized that something strange was happening. Suddenly, the youngest child bent over the pillow and screamed.

"What's the matter?" his brother asked.

"Look, look there!" he shouted.

Between the folds of their mother's nightgown was a small, dark ball. It was a raisin.

The children were frightened. The called louder and louder, "Mooooommy, mooooommy,...!"

Like the other times, there was no answer, but the oldest child realized that, with each shout, the raisin on the pillow moved slightly. They were quiet and watched it: the raisin didn't move. They shouted "Mom!" and the raisin shook a little.

Then they remembered their mother's words: "If this continues, I will shrink so much that you won't be able to see me." And, horrified, they realized that this raisin that moved when they yelled "Mom" was all that remained of their mother, who in that way tried to make them recognize her. How they cried and wailed!

"Poor us! What are we going to do now that Mom is a raisin? What is Dad going to say when he gets home and sees her?"

Their father had been on a business trip for several weeks, but was due to return home that very night. The children frightened and not knowing what to do, waited for him in their room all day long. Once in a while, to reassure themselves, they approached the raisin and called "Mom!" The raisin invariably moved.

That evening, their father arrived home. He opened the door, dropped his briefcase, took off his hat and coat, and called his wife from the hall: "Hello, are you there? Aren't you going to welcome me home? Aren't you going to give me a hug and bring me a glass of wine?"

Instead of his wife, his children appeared walking one behind the other with their heads bowed. The oldest held a matchbox in his hands.

"What's going on? Why aren't you in bed? And where's your mother?"

"She's in this box," the oldest answered in a mournful tone, "She turned into a raisin."

His father became angry, "You know that I hate jokes! Go to bed immediately!"

He searched the house for his wife. It was useless to tell him he would not find her. He then said, "She must have gone out for a walk!" But an hour later, as she had not appeared, he began to worry.

He put on his hat and left. He walked around the neighborhood, went to the houses of his neighbors, relatives and friends. He asked everyone, "Have you seen my wife?" Then he went to the police station. But they couldn't tell him anything either.

One night passed, a day and another night. And while the time passed and his wife continued to be missing, the father began to ask himself with great pain if his wife had died.

"She must have taken a walk by the lake and drowned! And the worst thing is, I will never know the truth!" he lamented in anguish.

The months passed with no news. Feeling very lonely, the man finally decided to remarry.

"A new wife would help me take care of these wild animals..."

So he chose a wife who was not as pretty as the first one—so as not to say frightful—but she seemed sweet and self-sacrificing. In reality, her face was as ugly as her heart was hard: she led him to believe that she adored the children, but the truth is that she detested them.

The father didn't realize anything. But the three children immediately understood that their stepmother was evil, and they did not trust her. Also, they knew that their real mother was still alive in the matchbox that they guarded so carefully. They were certain she would stop being a raisin and return to her former self.

From time to time at night, the children circled the box, removed the cover and called softly, "Mom, Mom."

And each time, the raisin responded by rocking gently.

One day when their father was in a good mood, they again asked him to go to their room to see what happened with the raisin. Perhaps he would understand! But their father didn't want to know anything; on the contrary, he became furious: "How long is this stupid joke going to continue? Little devils...if you keep up these stories, you are going to get it. I don't want to hear you mention that raisin again!"

Frightened, the children watched over the box.

But, horrors, the stepmother overheard the conversation from behind the door, and she believed them! For a while, she had had her suspicions about the match box that the children watched over with such anxiety.

At the beginning, she didn't say anything. But a few days later, one afternoon when the father wasn't home, she called the children and said to them: "Children, I am going to make a raisin cake and I am short one raisin. I believe you have one. Go get it right now!" The stepmother had an evil expression on her face. The children didn't dare protest. They went to their room and asked each other, "What should we do? We can't give her our mother so she can throw her in the oven!" The oldest decided, "Let's go up to the attic. We will hide the box and tell our step-mother that we lost it."

Unfortunately, the evil woman had followed them and once again listened to their conversation from behind the door. She entered the room like a whirlwind and yelled, "Don't you dare trick me! Give me the raisin now, I already have the oven hot!"

The oldest child had just enough time to grab the box. He yelled for his brothers to follow him, and ran upstairs as fast as he could. On his way out, he pushed the stepmother, who fell to the floor with a loud rattling of her bones because she was very thin.

The children ran up to the attic, closed the door and blocked the entrance with a large bureau. Meanwhile, the stepmother got up painfully, brushed herself off, and quickly headed toward the attic. "Open the door, brats! Open it up, little monsters! You'll see what will happen when your father gets home!" But the children, mute with fear, didn't budge.

Then, a cold, wicked and terrible fury invaded her.

"You don't want to open the door? Very well, you will stay locked there as long as it takes. And when you are dying from hunger. . .you will eat the raisin!" She took a key from her pocket and turned it in the lock. Then she laughed three times, "Ha, ha, ha," with a sharp and evil crackle that was unlike the musical laughs she let her husband hear.

At nightfall, her husband came home and asked, "Where are

the children?"

She answered, feigning surprise, "Don't you remember? They left to visit their grandmother in the country for a few days." She lied so convincingly that he said, distracted, "That's true, I had forgotten."

Meanwhile, above in the attic, the three children celebrated the victory of having escaped from the cruel woman. But as the hours passed and they became tired of being prisoners, they began to think about how they would escape. The only opening besides the sealed door was a small skylight that was difficult to reach since it was high above the floor in the rafters. And it was at least ten meters above the ground, over the garden.

"We could never jump," they said, "We would need a parachute or a rope."

But in the attic, they couldn't find anything. Suddenly, in the middle of their reflections, the three children realized with surprise that they hadn't fought, whined or played pranks for a long time. It was possible for them to behave! They were so happy with this discovery that they hugged each other and promised to continue their good behavior as long as they could.

But now it was vital that they find a way to escape. Night was falling and, with it, they felt the first signs of cold and hunger. The oldest sighed, "If only I had my bed and a good blanket." "And a large glass of warm milk," added the second. "And our beautiful mother," murmured the youngest. Not knowing what else to do, the children curled up on the floor in a corner, cuddling each other, with the matchbox in the middle. They stayed like that until they fell asleep.

In the morning, the growling of their stomachs woke them. They had never been so hungry before. "We must eat something!" they said. Then they looked at the matchbox. "Oh no," said the oldest, "we are not going to eat the raisin, never!" After thinking for a moment, he continued in a serious tone, "Brothers, remember the stories of lost explorers or shipwrecked people who are left without food? They end up eating anything or anyone... This must not happen to us!"

The youngest then said, "Let's separate ourselves from our mother so we can be sure we will not eat her."

"Yes," said the middle child, "If we throw her from the skylight, she will land on the grass in the garden and, since it is soft, she won't get hurt."

The children looked at the small raisin for the last time. Their eyes filled with tears. It was hard for them to separate from their mother!

But, how could they reach the skylight to throw her into the garden? They could drag over the bureau that was against the door and climb on top of it, but they ran the risk that the evil stepmother would choose that moment to search for them. No! The best thing was to try to climb on top of each other to reach the skylight. The oldest would stand on a chair, the middle child would balance on the very top and open the skylight.

And that is what they did. Or, it is what they almost did, because the chair was broken, which did not help the operation.

"Can you reach it? Can you touch the skylight?" the older children asked the youngest, who was balancing on top of them.

"Yes..., I found it...pass me the box!"

"What? Don't you have it?"

"No! I left it on the floor..."

They had to start over!

There was a small argument: each accused the other of having forgotten the box. But they soon made up.

"We'll just begin again," said the oldest child.

And they climbed on top of each other again: the oldest on the chair, the middle child on top of the oldest, and the youngest on top of the middle child, like acrobats. The youngest child reached the window and was about to open it when suddenly, crack, the chair broke in two and the children fell to the floor with a great crash.

At that very moment their father was entering the house. He heard the noise and said to his wife, "Go see what is happening!"

She disappeared for a moment and returned saying, "It isn't anything, just some mice running through the attic."

Meanwhile, in the attic, the three children were crying. Large tears of pain ran down their cheeks: tears of pain, because they had hurt themselves in the fall, and of frustration, because how were they going to reach the skylight now that the chair was broken? To console themselves, they opened the matchbox and looked at the raisin. But just seeing the raisin made them even sadder and they started to cry over it as hard as they could.

The children's tears fell in torrents on the matchbox, so that it flooded and the raisin was left floating in a small, warm puddle.

Suddenly, the oldest child shouted, "Look! It's growing!"

It was true. The raisin, swollen from the children's tears, had begun to grow. The more they cried, the more the raisin grew. And, seeing it grow, the children cried more, but now from happiness.

The raisin continued inflating, stretching, enlarging, growing more and more. Until...before the children's disbelieving eyes, it changed form and...

"Mommmmmmmm!" they yelled.

It was their mother, as tall and as beautiful as before she had shriveled up. The mother took her children in her arms and, laughing and crying, hugged them against her for a long time.

Meanwhile, on the first floor, the father was wondering about the strange noises that were coming from the attic. Finally, he could stand it no longer and he said to his wife, "Those mice in the attic have a strange way of squeaking. It is as if they were crying. Give me the keys...I am going to see what is happening."

His wife tried every way to stop him, but her efforts were in vain. He went upstairs, tried to open the door with the key and, when it wouldn't open, pushed it with all his might. Imagine his surprise to find his three children in the arms of his first, beautiful wife! The four, hugging tightly, looked at him without saying anything.

Then this man, who wasn't as bad as he seemed, felt as if he would die from remorse and joy. He covered his children with kisses and then, kneeling at his wife's feet, he begged forgiveness for having doubted her.

He was immediately forgiven, and father, mother and children walked downstairs hand-in-hand to have dinner, with their hearts full of happiness.

The stepmother hadn't waited for them. Guessing what had happened, she had run off at full speed with her bags.

The raisin cake in the oven was completely burnt.

The mother threw it in the trash and quickly made another, delicious cake full of candied fruit.

The whole family happily and hungrily ate this new cake that didn't contain a single raisin.

Translated by Janice Molloy

The Beguiling Ladies

The Servants' Slaves

Silvina Ocampo

Herminia Berni was really lovely. I just do not believe that hers was simply an inner beauty, as some people used to say, though if you looked closely she did have a few faults: she squinted slightly, her lips were far too thick, her cheeks were sunken, her hair was utterly lank. But without a doubt, she could have been Miss Argentina. Beauty is a strange thing. Herminia was lovely and her mistress adored her.

"The mistress is a very dear lady," she told me when I went to the house to visit.

I looked at her in amazement. She was not only pretty, she was good too. I never imagined she might be a hypocrite. There was mutual affection between the lady of the house and the maid, as I discovered later.

On that day, when I went to the house for the first time, I stumbled over a stuffed tiger and broke a china sweet dish. Herminia religiously collected all the pieces of the broken dish and put them safely into a box in tissue paper. She could not bear anyone breaking her mistress' ornaments. Her mistress had been ill, seriously ill, for some three months. The house was filled with cards, telegrams, flowers and plants which friends had sent to her.

"Only a corpse receives that many sprays," commented one of the visitors, who was even jealous of illness. She would not even go back home to sleep, for fear of missing any of the presents sent to the sick woman. She wanted to enjoy all the advantages every bit as much as the sufferings of her friend.

"It's not healthy to breathe the scent of all these flowers," said another woman, taking the best roses away with her.

"I think it's all very tactless. Why don't they send her a night-dress, or a dressing gown or some sweets, nice milky caramels that she likes so much?" said another woman, without looking up from her knitting.

"Flowers get on my nerves. What she needs are artificial ones, the real-looking kind, though, not painted ones," said another woman, who was being very nice to Herminia.

To tell the truth, they were all very nice to Herminia and there was a good reason for it. When they saw her looking so thin and faded, making herself so upset by her mistress' illness, the visitors used to bring her chocolate in a box with painted cats, or nourishing little cakes in a little plastic basket, or tarts with quince jam inside, in a little case that had Bon Voyage written on it, or orange jelly in a glass powder bowl with the odd flaw in it. The could not bear to see her so run down.

"You must look after yourself," they used to say to her.

"I'd rather die," she would retort, without telling any lies.

Her faithfulness was a model, but the affection which Señora de Bersi lavished upon her was a model too. In her room that was crammed with paintings, there in a place of honor was a portrait of Herminia in fancy dress.

She would have allowed her to talk on the phone whenever she liked, to go out at night, to whistle or sing while she was cleaning the rooms, to sit and watch TV in the sitting room with a ciga-rette in her mouth, but Herminia never did anything like that.

"She's not a very modern sort of girl," said one visitor to another.

Gradually I began to realize that all those women were actually going round to visit Herminia, nor Señora de Bersi. They didn't try to hide it and every time I would surprise them saying:

"We're slaves to our own servants, let's admit it."

"My girl left me."

Or:

"The girl I've got is awful."

Or even:

"I'm trying to find a girl, but she must have references."

"Herminia is a gem."

They went to visit Herminia in the hope of finding themselves alone with her, to say more or less these words to her, which they had carefully prepared:

"Herminia, when Señora de Bersi dies, and God forbid that should happen, but things do, you know, I sometimes ask myself whether you would come and work in my house. You'd have a room of your own, you could have every Sunday and holiday free, of course. I'd treat you like my own daughter, and believe me, there wouldn't be nearly so much for you to do, much less than you do here. These rooms are very big, there are so many stairs and brushing all these stuffed animals must be hard work. You're strong, but you never know if it's wise to put yourself under so much strain. Obviously in my house you would be expected to do a little sewing, some washing, cooking, cleaning the courtyard, some ironing, taking the dog out three times a day and bathing it once a week, and drying it and grooming it, but these are all trivial jobs that only take a few minutes to do. In fact, you'd really have nothing to do at all."

Herminia enjoyed working in Señora de Bersi's house. The stuffed tiger had its own special toothbrush, and there was a special brush for the piano keys too. There was a special sponge for the marble cupid, and a little brush for cleaning the silver doves. She was upset when the visitors talked in such a offensive way. "One of these days I'll send them all to the devil; they're fussing as if it were me that was ill."

Tuco, Señora de Bersi's eldest son, who was married and very fond of music, used to prowl around the piano. Once Herminia saw him measure the piano with a tape. Such strange behaviour did not bode well. Did he want to take away the piano himself? Herminia became twice as watchful. She stationed herself close to the piano, when she was darning or adding up her shopping lists, but one day the Señora's son took her by the hand and said: "Why don't you come with me, honey?"

Faced with this monstrous proposition, Herminia pretended to be deaf and did not reply. But the interest that Señor Tuco showed in the piano did not relax, and Herminia returned to find him with a tape measure noting down the measurements of the piano in a little green book that he took out of his pocket. Herminia did not sleep, but her watchfulness was doomed to failure. She had to keep going out to buy things or to pay bills and on one of these occasions her worst fears were realized: guilty hands removed the piano. Herminia was deeply upset by the loss of the piano, with its candlesticks and its bronze pedals, but then something unexpected happened. Tuco, who had personally overseen the removal of the piano by stealth, assisted by two odd job men, paid dearly for his daring betrayal. Apart from being a good for nothing, he was a weak man and the effort was obviously far too great for him. Just as he was descending the last step in the house, he stumbled and died under the weight of the piano. Herminia had to give her mistress the news. Not one tear did Señora de Bersi shed when she heard about Tuco's death. Herminia was so very tactful, even when bringing bad news. She was a real gem.

Señora Alma Monteson did not waste any time in offering Herminia a serious position as housekeeper or ladies' companion in her own home. She said they would travel to Europe and she would make all the arrangements, put everything neatly into the suitcases and pay all the fares for the most important places in Europe to which they would be going, in short, it would be a very pleasant life with none of the work she had always had to do, unpleasant jobs like washing, ironing and cleaning out rooms. Herminia was not in the least bit tempted by this offer, and replied angrily: "I won't abandon Señora de Bersi for any reason on earth."

"But you must see that Señora de Bersi is very ill and what she really needs is a nurse, not a maid like you, who is just wasting her life shut up in here."

Herminia turned her back on her and did not say one more word. The next day, the papers carried the news that Señora Alma Monteson had died suddenly of a heart attack.

Lilian Guevara, a distant relation of Señora de Bersi who had recently married, visited her several times to see how she was getting along, and one day she offered Herminia a job. She was shy and it took a lot of hesitating, clearing her throat and coughing before she said: "Herminia, I need a girl like you and as Señora de Bersi is so very sick, I'm sure she will end up dead before much longer, and I think you would get along very well in my house. I spend all my summers by the sea. I have a lovely home, you must have seen the photographs in *Ideal Home* or the feature in *La Nacion*. I'd take you with me and you could go down to the beach every morning for a swim. And in winter, when I go on one of my trips to Bariloche, I'd take you with me, because I don't like to be apart from my maids when they're as good as you are. Señora de Bersi has told me so often about how marvelous you are and I'd really, really like to have someone like you in my home.

Herminia was left stunned. She could not believe that this young woman had spoken to her in terms of such vulgarity. To stop herself crying, she burst into wild laughter. It was an awful moment, because her laughter could not appease anything. In that sorrowful, silent house Herminia's laughter seemed more tragic than all the tears of the hypocrites asking after Señora de Bersi's health. Afterwards, she went off quietly into a corner of the house to think, as though she were praying.

The news came on the radio that same night. Lilian Guevara had died in a car crash in the neighborhood of La Magdalena.

Señora de Bersi did not get any worse, nor did she get any better. Her state of health filled the house with uncertainty and heaviness, but she did not seem to be suffering too much and she was getting used to being an invalid, as some sick people do. The visitors, who grew more numerous every day, decided to ask a team of doctors to discuss the treatment that the sick woman needed.

So they called a well-known specialist and had him come over from La Plata, they called a heart specialist and a pediatrician who lived near Señora de Bersi's house and they waited for them all in the lobby in an anxious group, chatting as they did every afternoon in that house. The bravest of them, for there are always some brave women, decided to go and talk to the doctors before they all met together. Through the window they watched the arrival of these great men. From the window they saw them get out of their cars; cautiously they moved towards the door, waiting for the elevator to come up and then as though by chance they talked to the doctors at the end of the hall, when they were taking off their coats and mufflers.

One woman said:

"Doctor, don't you think it's..inhuman..to prolong the life of a lady who's suffering so much?"

Another said to one of the doctors:

"Tell me, doctor, couldn't you give her something to shorten her road to Calvary a little?"

And another said:

"If I were in her position, I'd honestly prefer to be given something to end my life once and for all."

Herminia was sitting close to the window watching all this. She did not like it, she did not like it at all that they wanted to take over her mistress' life, that so many frivolous women were wandering along the corridors of the house, sitting in the parlor, touching the books, the vases, the wild animals, stroking the fur of the señora's favorite animals. And it was still a sore point that the son had taken away the piano. Hadn't they forced the lock on one of the glass cabinets, where the fans and the ivory chessmen were displayed? What would happen next? How sad life is, thought Herminia. She would never have imagined that people could be so wicked, that friendship could be so false, that riches could be so useless. Tears fell from her eyes, and she explained: "There's some dust in my eye." Sighs fell from her lips, and she explained: "I have a cold in my chest." She was even reserved about her sorrow. The people who saw her looking so sad were more worried about her than they were about Señora de Bersi. The milkman who brought the milk, the bread-man with his huge basket of bread, the grocer all asked:

"How is Señorita Herminia? What's wrong with Señorita Herminia? Is Señorita Herminia sick?"

Lina Grundic, the piano teacher who once upon a time had taught Señora de Bersi to play the piano, seemed a serious person, seemed more reserved, seemed better than all the other ladies. One day she called Herminia and said: "Herminia, the fastening on my bodice has come unstitched. I don't like to bother you, but these breasts of mine would even arouse a statue. Could I trouble you for a needle and thread to sew it up?"

They went together to the bathroom. Herminia sat on the edge of the bathtub and sewed the fastening on the pianist's bodice, while she combed her hair in the mirror, dampened her hair to set in the waves, put on her lipstick and powdered her face. Neither of the two said a word. In the silence of the afternoon music could be heard, cheerful music coming from the house next door.

"How depressing it must be for you, Herminia," said the pianist softly, "living in this house, and you so young too. How many years have you been working for Señora de Bersi?"

"Eight," answered Herminia.

"You must have been very young when you first came here, nothing but a child."

"I don't think I was so young. Other girls of my age, friends of mine, had been working in other houses for five years already when I came to this one."

"You're a real gem, and like all real gems you need airing. Do you know what happens to real gems if they stay shut up for too long? They lose their shine and nothing can put it back again, absolutely nothing."

"There are all sorts of modern inventions to make they shiny again."

"No there aren't, modern inventions aren't enough, nor are eight rooms. But in any case, it all seems very depressing to me. Don't you want to go to new places, to travel and get to know the world?

I don't know, but I imagine that someone as young as you are must take an interest in life."

"I've never thought about it," answered Herminia.

"I'd like to have someone like you in my house. I've been invited to the United States, to the Chicago Conservatory to give some concerts. Sometimes they invite me to France or Italy. I'd like you with me. Now why are you blushing, sweetie?"

Herminia's heart beat fast. Even this woman was betraying Señora de Bersi. She snapped her sewing thread with her teeth and handed back the black bodice, stuffed with artificial feathers, to the pianist. Then without saying a word, she went out of the bathroom and locked the door.

A week later they found the pianist, Lina Grundic, dead in the elevator in her house. The mystery of her death remained unsolved. Nobody knew if it was a question of suicide or murder.

Herminia, who sometimes called herself Arminda, seemed much calmer. The visitors did not come to the house quite so often. To tell the truth, they were afraid of ending up like the unfortunate Alma Monteson, or Tuco Bersi, or Lina Grundic or Lilian Guevara. The days seemed happier and Señora de Bersi looked much better, she was more cheerful and she chatted as she had not chatted for a long time. In fact it seemed that her life was going to go on and on, and that some day she would appear in the newspapers as one of those ladies who has reached her 110th or 120th birthday and who are photographed with a short life story and details of how they managed to stay well enough to reach such an advanced age, what sort of diet they kept to, what kind of water they drank, how long did they sleep and how many hours a week did they play cards. And this miracle of longevity was all due to Herminia, as she herself admitted to the journalists: "May the lord grant Herminia everything she asks for. She's a real gem. She's prolonged my life for me."

Translated by Susan Bassnett

The Beguiling Ladies

Elvira Orphée

It happened a while back, when the town was neither as big as now nor as given to reading. Only the men read the newspapers and they told the women, who didn't understand all that much about it and were annoyed when the found themselves pursued throughout the house by that sort of nattering while they were trying to work.

In the pension of dona Eulogia, only two young men remained when she died without heirs. They both worked at the Post Office, and, as they had come from the other side of the mountains some time before, for all practical purposes had no family.

Dona Eulogia's house was lovely, so lovely that no one would even think of leaving it to go out for a night on the town. Over the years, she had gone along remodeling and expanding it as she took in more and more boarders, with each new addition responding to her fancy of the moment. Every so often, the house as a whole seemed to acquire an appearance completely different from that of its older parts. But dona Eulogia herself was like that—she might dress all in black or cover herself with gee-gaws and necklaces when she had visitors—but she was still always dona Eulogia beneath the lace and frippery, and likewise the house, though facaded with different fantasies, always remained itself in the end. It was simply that it changed so from time to time that it proved diverting, enchanting, made it difficult to leave behind.

From the dead woman, the young men had picked up her way of ordering things, her eccentricities, and that notion of being different one day to the next. It occurred to them to put out some plants in a way nobody had ever thought of: wisteria and swallowwort covering an entire corner of the garden. They put the swallowwort in baskets woven of mesh they made themselves, so fine it was invisible, which they then hung. The swallowwort, velvety beige, peeked through the wisteria like little stars born out of air. Then they wanted a flower, one also beige, the color of wrapping paper, velvety too. And they acquired it, by complicated manipulations of grafts. They mixed it among the wisteria in the corner, and they also planted it in the earth, amidst the Paraguayan jasmines with their flowers that look like sisters who have fallen out, some so white and others so violet.

If the young men had not been so friendly, just like dona Eulogia had been, people might have found them rather peculiar. For dona Eulogia, just about any occasion was a good one for sending out for some pasteries, serving a spot of liqueur, and gathering in the front patio. It was even better if she could scare up somebody to sing. Even at the point when she was really too sick to get up, she celebrated the birth of some kittens with empanadas and lime aspic. She had the neighbors called, and to the best among them she presented some of the kittens with the charge that they take good care of them. She finally went to sleep the siesta about four o'clock, by which time here eyes were already heavy from tippling.

The young men were not drinkers, but they were so fond of dona Eulogia that to humor her they would join her in a drink now and then. She had found girlfriends for the both of them, and if nothing much came of it, it was because they were doing just fine where they were, and they knew, surely, that there was no other place where they were going to have such a good time as in that house where the maid herself was caught up in the fanci-fulness and made strangely mixed sweets that even the local phar-macist (Russian and a master of candies) envied.

With dona Eulogia dead and the flowers on the patio woven like a tapestry, the young men turned their attention to the furni-ture. It was pretty, but a bit uninspired and of a uniform sobriety. They had brought in some carpenters and fiddled around strip-ping varnish and planing down the wood, when one day an adver-tisement in the newspaper leapt out at them: *Come to #16 Ronco Mot, and you will find the table and buffet that you always desired. The one you have seen in your dreams.*

Next day the two were so utterly careless vending stamps that they might have given them away if people hadn't been pressing money into their hands. They exchanged suppositions in low voice: Would that furniture really be so dreamy? Because when they dreamed, it was no small potatoes! It wasn't for nothing they were living in dona Eulogia's house, itself so like a dream hidden right in the middle of town, a house that would vanish if its residents failed to respect its laws and customs.

They left the post office, not running so as to avoid gossip, but with a gait that set their ties flapping like flags.

As they were running out of city and almost out of daylight, they regretted not having taken a bus. With their predilection for dreams, they'd had greater faith in their legs than in wheels. Now, they were walking along streets where there were no sidewalks and eucaplytus trees threatened to block the way, when suddenly they saw again a sidewalk and a facade with two balconies, not too far from a train station. The stoop of the house was very clean; the door had windows of beveled glass so spotless they could have fooled a fly. An old woman opened the door, her hands crossed, hidden in her sleeves, and her gaze a bit downcast. Inside, the house seemed just like any other, and the young men were feeling more than a bit disillusioned when they entered a room which astounded them. There was that buffet of their dreams, just as the advertise-ment promised, of a blond wood, rounded on the sides and deco-rated along the edges with little flowers of extremely fine colored poreclain. And, even more incredibly, it hung from the wall. They were so mesmerized by it they failed to notice two other ladies quite similar in appearance to the one who had opened the door for them. One might even have had a hat on. But the young men now were looking at a round table, gorgeous, white but not really white completely because it was made of tiny squares, some tinged with gray, others with yellow, all shimmering like marble. There were many marvels in the room, four porcelain tigers, suspended from the ceiling, supported a sheet of glass, upon which were artificial fruits made of wicker, copper, opal and onyx. It was now difficult to see much of anything. Night stole into the room, and one of the ladies said that they did not show their treasures except in the full light of day, for without sun, everything dies. The young men nearly cried. The old woman, as if filled with pity for them, proposed they remain the night *in unimaginable beds*, so as to avoid the need of making the trip again tomorrow. Anxious to see the beds, the young men agreed. The old ladies, in procession, guided them through this house of numberless rooms, and in one showed them a column of turned alabaster, so tall that it almost permitted one to see beneath the bed or platform it supported without ducking. That platform was transparent, and you'll soon know what it was made of. Without the young men noticing how (surely by means of a stairway, itself transparent, at the head), the most elegant of the old ladies climbed up and laid down upon the bed. The other two turned on lights underneath and all could see through the transparent. . .opal? Water trapped in soft glass? The silhouette of a rosy body, like when one puts a hand in front of the light and sees the color of blood. It was all very beautiful, even if, in the telling, it sounds like something which might be a little frightening for the young men. But they were enchanted. They were also pleased that the old ladies, up to that point a bit slow and sad, seemed to liven up and took out some liqueurs, like dona Eulogia.

The following day, they awoke very late and, embarrassed by the hour, felt they couldn't really go to work. Beyond that, the beds. rocking softly like hammocks, didn't much encourage popping right up to meet the day. The beds were not supported by columns of alabaster, as they had believed the night before, but very fine string intricately woven as lace and hung from the ceiling. The mattresses themselves were of a transparent rubber, filled with slightly warmed water.

When they finally got up, it was the middle of the afternoon, and they got to thinking of their plants and of that lovely anarchy of the house of doña Eulogia: a lonely hat on the piano as if someone had just departed, having left a final note lingering in the air; her cabinets of fans and silk ruffles that, at best, doña Eulogia herself had tatted but that she identified as the pledge of a lovesick poet (which perhaps was true). They thought of all this and, too, that the house of these old lady furniture sellers, aside from the furniture itself, really was nothing extraordinary. And if it were true that these were the furnishings of your dreams, they were as well those of your nightmares, as the suspended beds which last night had so fascinated now repelled them with those little tubes of reddish water, like some cheap circus trick. They thus limited their discussion of possible purchases to the blond wood cabinet, the tiger table, and of another piece, truly out of a dream, bright with golds, browns, and touches of red, that the women referred to as the autumn chest. By the time they were ready to go, they discovered it was already night. The women said, no, no, you can't go now, these streets are so dark, with who knows what maniac on the loose in these parts, and why hurry away? One of them suggested that the hanging beds had not been to their liking and proposed they sleep in others *so beautiful as to make you dream the dreams you most desire.* The idea of seeing those beds conquered both young men, and when they gazed on them, they were thunderstruck: their form was that of a bed, but these were made of things that for bed-making, would never have occurred to anyone—lacquered turtle shells, polished horn, something like caramel that they could not identify and that the old women chose not to name. The young men lost all desire to go, though they did insist that, this evening, there be no partying, for they really had to get to work the following day. The old ladies accepted that condition.

Next morning, when they were bidding them good-bye, they kept their eyes down. They did not accompany the young men to the threshold. When that door opened, there stood an immense black dog with fur like sheep's wool that froze them right on the doorsill. Every move they made toward leaving was mirrored by the dog.

The young men despaired. Even now, they would arrive late for work. It was difficult to ask the offended old ladies to do something about the dog. There was no other way out. The ladies said that the dog wasn't theirs and didn't obey them, that it wouldn't let even them leave when it was around unless it wanted to. Finally, overcome with their anxiousness to be gone, the young men thought of getting away by climbing the back fence. Horror pulled them up short when they reached the back patio. Beyond a spindly little gate and flimsy wire were animals so bizarre they seemed escaped from the Temptation of St. Anthony. That hog...A hog with an elephant's trunk, or was it a dwarf elephant? And that one? A dogcat or a catdog? Whatever they were, they were utterly silent. They were all mute.

The hearts of the young men swam tremulously, fibrillating, shivering like terrified meat. They lost all control. They tried to climb the high walls surrounding the house, hoping to reach the balcony which, they discovered, was blocked by a door of quebracho wood secured with a padlock. All they could do now was sleep as many nights in the house as the old ladies wished.

Sometimes, touching those silken furnishings, they forgot they were prisoners, and others, they recalled that astonishing house of dona Eulogia as if it were paradise. One fine day, sadly, they understood that the lost paradise of their memories had lacked the beauty of beautiful animals: inoffensive tigers, endowed with language, living alongside stags, ever the victims, lambs to the slaughter; herons enamored of flamingos; harmonious interbreedings of turtles and roosters, to the point of producing an animal that, disloyal to either progenitor, shimmered with the splendor of tortise shell and feathers. The old ladies had achieved none of this in their crossbreedings, for the lack of experience and the accidental nature of it all. They had only managed something similar in that beautiful furniture.

The old women continued to be very hospitable, without saying anything to the young men about what it was they had in mind for them. But given that they shared with the young men a passion for the unexpected recombinations of beauty, the young men knew that they were being held prisoner in order to make beautiful things out of living ones. Except, were they more knowledgeable of that kind of grafting than the old ladies? A particular perplexity stole over them: Regarding Eve in Paradise—had she not served to simplify things rather than produce beautiful combinations?

With their liqueurs far different than the innocent ones of dona Eulogia, the old ladies were drying out the young men's brains. And meanwhile, the house of dona Eulogia grew more and more sad in the hands of the servant, and the servant herself grew sad from loneliness. I remembered the advertisement about the furniture, recalling how anxious the boys were to go and see about it, and that it was at that time that they disappeared. But I couldn't recollect the address, and I said nothing to the people who made inquiries so as not to muddy my own situation or draw any blame onto myself.

Even half-stupefied, the boys realized how well the old ladies worked with herbs and pulverized stones. If not, they couldn't have come within a whiff of producing such peculiar animals. And when the ladies gave them their potions, powders and shared what they already had discovered, the young men even found themselves vaguely pleased with the idea that they would soon be inventing marvelous animals. Afterwards came nights of socializing with the old ladies which left them exhausted, sleeping two or three days running. During these times, they would be waited upon by servants almost children, beautiful but oddly vacant. There were blond ones, with short, wiry hair like a negro's and full, heavy lips, with the eagle beak noses of the Andes, with violet eyes and skin white as flour; others had long hair, straight and dark, with green, slanting eyes. The combinations were so various not all come to mind, and so much time has passed I may have forgotten some of them.

These little girls followed in the young men's footsteps all day. But the poor things really didn't have a chance. Perhaps if they had made themselves a bit more sociable, or if the boys themselves had had some stronger inclinations in that direction. But I suspect they were born pretty limited in that department, made more for the role of favorite son than cock of the walk. Beyond that, the little girls seemed more like mobile dolls, so different from dona Eulogia, always so animated. Too, the young men found themselves wondering one day (perhaps when they arose with their inclinations a bit awakened) if those powders and potions that the old women gave to them to invent new animals were also being slipped into those spots of liqueur. And then it all became clear: the animals were only the trials for the human experiments. And the old ladies had already done it. With whom? They themselves when they were young, possibly, along with some fellow interested in furniture. Although, who could be sure, with those potions, if the old ladies still didn't have some aspirations where the present young men were concerned? The upshot of it all was that this realization popped the cork of the young men's fear, and the house of dona Eulogia called them so powerfully it must have been dona Eulogia herself that spurred them on, she and her innocent get-togethers, her extravagant but so decent fantasies, her happiness and generosity. One of them realized suddenly: that dog at the door is crossed with sheep, that's why his head is so peculiar. It approached them not with malice but curiosity. With absolute decision he took the other young man by the hand and led him out to the street, without even worrying if the old ladies were offended or not. The dog hardly sniffed at them before it began to baah. They discovered anew the legs which had brought them there almost at a run; and they arrived exhausted and without a cent at the house of dona Eulogia.

They did not tell the entire truth to those who inquired (it's common knowledge these types figure everybody for a sneak and a thief). But to me, they told everything. And I believed it all, even more so when, throughout the city, monsters began to appear all over town, terrifying people to the point we were suffering from epidemics of terror. The boys went around pleased as punch thinking about how the old ladies would be scared they'd expose them. They lost their jobs at the Post Office, found a carpenter to apprentice themselves to, and you really have to see the furniture they were making in just a short time. But only for a very select clientele.

Translated by Christopher Leland

The Museum of Futile Endeavours

Cristina Peri Rossi

Every afternoon I visit the Museum of Futile Endeavours. I request the catalogue and sit at the large wooden table. The pages of the catalogue are somewhat faded, but I like to browse through them slowly, as if leafing through time. I never see anyone reading; this must be why the woman who work there pays me so much attention. Since I am one of the few visitors, she spoils me. She must be afraid of losing her job for lack of patrons. Before I go inside, I look carefully at the printed sign which hangs from the glass door. It says: "Hours: Mornings, 9-2. Evenings: 5-8. Mondays, closed." Although I always know which Futile Endeavour I want to look up, I ask for the catalogue anyway so that the girl will have something to do.

"What year do you want?" she asks me attentively.

"The 1922 catalogue," I answer, for example.

She appears shortly with a thick book bound in Cordovan leather and places it on the table opposite my chair. She is very kind, and if she thinks that the light coming through the window is insufficient, she herself turns on the bronze lamp with the green tulip shade and arranges it so that its light falls upon the pages of my book. Sometimes, when I return the catalogue, I address a brief remark to her. I tell her, for example:

"1922 was a very intensive year. Many people undertook futile endeavours. How many volumes are there?"

"Fourteen," she answers very professionally.

And I note one of the futile endeavors of that year, children who tried to fly, men determined to become rich, complicated contraptions which never worked, many lovers.

"The year 1975 was much richer," she tells me a little sadly. "We still haven't recorded all the entries."

"The cataloguers must be very busy," I reflect aloud.

"Oh, yes," she answers. "They have just gotten to the letter C and there are already several volumes published. And that's not counting the repeats."

It's very curious that futile endeavours are repeated, but the repetitions are not included in the catalogue: they would take up too much room. A man tried to fly seven times, using different devices; some prostitutes tried to change their profession; a woman wanted to paint a picture; someone tried to overcome fear; almost all attempted to become immortal or lived as if they were.

The clerk assures me that only a minuscule part of the futile endeavours ever reaches the museum. In the first place, the administration is short of funds, and they can scarcely make any purchases or exchanges, or disseminate the work of the museum to the provinces or abroad; in the second place, the exorbitant quantity of futile endeavours which are continuously realized would mean that many people would have to work without hope of compensation or public recognition. Occasionally, despairing of public support, they have appealed to private initiative, but the results have been insignificant and discouraging. Virginia—that is the name of the charming clerk at the museum who is the habit of talking with me—tells me that the private sources they appealed to always turned out to be very demanding and uncomprehending, and misrepresented the purpose of the museum.

The building stands on the outskirts of the city, in a wasteland full of cats and rubbish, where one can still find, just below the surface of the earth, cannon balls from an ancient war, the pommels of rusty swords, the jaw bones of an ass eaten away by time.

"Do you have a cigarette?" Virginia asks me with a gesture which does not quite hide her anxiety.

I search my pockets. I find an old key, slightly nicked, the tip of a broken screw driver, my return bus ticket, a shirt button, some loose change, and at last, two crushed cigarettes. She smokes furtively, hidden by the thick volumes with peeling spines, the wall clock which is always wrong (usually slow), and the old dusty moldings. It is believed that there, on the site of the museum, a wartime fortification once stood. The heavy stones of the foundation and several beams were salvaged, and the walls were shored up. The museum was inaugurated in 1946. Some photographs of the ceremony have survived, with men in morning coats and ladies in long, dark dresses, rhinestone jewelry, and hats decorated with birds or flowers. One can imagine an orchestra playing ballroom music in the distance; the guests have a half-solemn, half-ridiculous look about them as someone cuts a cake decorated with an official ribbon.

I neglected to say that Virginia is slightly squint-eyed. This little defect gives her face a comic touch that softens her ingenuousness, as if her deflected gaze were a humorous comment floating detached from context.

The Futile Endeavours are arranged alphabetically. When the letters are used up, numbers are added. The system is long and complicated. Each one has a pigeon hole, its own page, and own description. Walking among them with extraordinary gracefulness, Virginia looks like a priestess, the virgin of an ancient cult removed from time.

Several of the Futile Endeavours are beautiful; others, somber. We are not always in agreement on their classification.

Leafing through a volume, I found one about a man who for ten years had tried to teach his dog to speak. And another man, who spent more than twenty years trying to win a woman's heart. He would bring her flowers, plants, butterfly catalogues, he would offer her trips, he composed poems, wrote songs, built a house, forgave all her mistakes, tolerated her lovers and then he killed himself.

"It was an arduous undertaking," I say to Virginia. "But possibly stimulating."

"It is a somber story," Virginia answers. "The museum has a complete description of this woman. She was a frivolous, fickle, unfaithful, lazy and resentful creature. Her understanding left much to be desired and she was also selfish."

There are men who have made long journeys seeking places which did not exist, unrecoverable memories, women who died and friends who disappeared. There are children who undertook impossible tasks with great fervor. Like the ones who would dig a hole which was continually filled in with water.

In the museum, smoking is not allowed, nor is singing. The latter restriction seems to affect Virginia as much as the former.

"I would like to sing a little tune once in a while," she allows, wistfully.

People whose futile endeavor consisted of attempting to trace their family tree, prospecting for gold, writing a book. Others hoped to win the lottery.

"The travelers are my favorites," Virginia tells me.

Entire sections of the museum are dedicated to these journeys. We reconstruct them on the pages of books. After wandering for some time across diverse seas, traversing dark forests, visiting cities and markets, crossing bridges, sleeping on trains or on benches at the station, they forget the purpose of their journey and nevertheless they keep on traveling. One day they disappear without a trace or a memory, swept away in a flood, trapped in a tunnel or asleep forever in a doorway. No one claims them.

Before, Virginia tells me, there were a few private researchers; amateurs who contributed material to the museum. I can even remember a time when collecting Futile Endeavours was fashionable, like philately or ant farms.

"I think the abundance of material ruined the hobby," Virginia declared. "It's only stimulating to look for what's scarce, to find what's rare."

In those days they would come to the museum from distant parts, ask for information, become interested in some case, leave with pamphlets and return laden with stories, which they would publish, along with the corresponding photographs. Futile endeavours that they brought to the museum, like butterflies, or strange insects. For example, the story of the man who spent five years determined to prevent a war, until one day the first bullet fired by a mortar blew off his head. Or Lewis Carroll, who spent his life avoiding drafts and died of a cold the one time he forgot his raincoat.

I don't know if I mentioned that Virginia is slightly squint-eyed. I frequently amuse myself trying to follow the direction of that gaze that goes I don't know where. When I see her cross the hall, burdened with pamphlets, tomes, all kinds of documents, I cannot help getting up and going to help her.

Sometimes, in the middle of a task, she complains a little.

"I'm tired of coming and going," she says. "We will never finish classifying everything. And the newspapers, too. They are full of futile endeavours."

Like the story of the boxer who tried to recover his title five times, until he was disqualified because of a bad blow to his eye. Now, he surely wanders from cafe to cafe, in some sordid section of the city, remembering when he could see well and his fists were deadly. Or the story of the trapeze artist who suffered from vertigo, and couldn't look down. Or the dwarf who wanted to grow and went everywhere looking for a doctor to cure him.

When she's tired of moving volumes she sits down on a pile of old, dusty newspapers, and smokes a cigarette—furtively, because it's not permitted—and muses aloud.

"We might have to hire someone else," she says with resignation.

Or: "I don't know when they'll pay me this month's salary."

I have asked her to go for a walk with me in the city, have coffee, or go to the movies. But she has refused. She will only talk to me within the grey and dusty walls of the museum.

If time passes, I'm not aware of it, occupied as I am every afternoon. But Mondays are days of discomfort and abstinence, when

I don't know what to do, or how to live.

The museum closes at eight o'clock in the evening. Virginia herself puts the simple metal key in the lock, without taking any further precautions, since no one would try to break into the museum. Only once did anyone try to break in, Virginia tells me—a man who wanted to erase his name from the catalogue. As an adolescent he had undertaken a futile endeavour, and now he was ashamed of it, and didn't want any trace to remain.

"We discovered him in time," Virginia says. "It was very difficult to dissuade him. He insisted on the private nature of his endeavour, and wanted us to return it to him. On that occasion, I was very firm and decisive. It was a rare piece, almost a collector's item, and the museum would have suffered a serious loss if this man had gotten his way."

When the museum closes, I leave it with a sense of melancholy. At first the time that had to pass until the next day seemed intolerable to me. But I learned to wait. I have also become accustomed to Virginia's presence, and without her, the existence of the museum would seem impossible. I know that the director also thinks so (that one, the man in the photograph with the two-colored sash on his chest), since he's decided to promote her. Because there is no echelon prescribed by law or custom, he has invented a new position, which is really the same one, but now it has another title. He has named her vestal of the temple, not without reminding her of the sacred nature of her mission—to guard, at the entrance of the museum, the fleeting memory of the living.

Translated by Alison Weber

The Authors

HELENA ARAUJO (Colombia, 1930), a novelist and literary critic, resides in Laussane where she teaches Latin American literature written by women. She is the author of *La Sheherazade Criolla*.

DORA ALONSO (Cuba, 1910) has written two novels, *Tierra Adentro* (1944) and *Tierra inerme* (1961) as well as numerous short stories, plays, and children's books. Since 1946 she has written for Cuban national radio and television.

JACQUELINE BALCELLS (Chile, 1945) is one of Chile's most promising writers of short stories for children.

YOLANDA BEGREGAL (Bolivia, 1916) is the author of many novels, including *Almadia* and *Bajo el Oscuro Sol*, and she is considered to be Bolivia's most outstanding poet.

PATRICIA BINS (Brazil, 1942) is a prominent painter and journalist, as well as novelist. The author of four novels as well as a collection of short stories, she is well-known for intimate portraits of her female protagonists. *Janela de Sonho* (1986) is among her most recent novels.

MARIÁ LUISA BOMBAL (Chile, 1910-1980) is one of Latin America's most outstanding writers. A traveler since childhood, she spent her youth in Paris, then moved to Buenos Aires and New York before returning to Chile in 1972. Her novels, *La Ultima Niebla* (1933) and *La Amortajada*, are considered to be among the most artfully crafted narratives in Chilean literature because of their lyrical qualities.

MARTA BRUNET (Chile, 1897-1967) is, along with Bombal, considered to be a most outstanding Chilean writer. Her work depicts with clarity the situation of rural women in Chile. She is the author of numerous collections of short stories as well as novels.

MARGO GLANTZ (Mexico, 1930) is a novelist, journalist, and professor at the National University of Mexico. She has been instrumental in founding journals and establishing television shows in her native country. She is the author of numerous novels as well as critical writings. The excerpt published here is from her most recent book, *Genealogies*, already in its fifth printing.

HILDA HILST (Brazil, 1930) is a poet, playwright, and fiction writer. Her works include *Fluxofloema*, *Qados*, and *Ficcoes*.

CLARICE LISPECTOR (Brazil, 1925-1977) has come to be considered the most important woman writer in contemporary Brazilian letters. The author of seven novels and short-story collections as well as children's books, her translated work has gained her a strong international reputation. A collection of her stories, *Soulstorm*, translated by Alexis Levitin, was recently published by New Directions.

CARMEN NARANJO (Costa Rica, 1930) is a former ambassador

to Israel and Minister of Culture. An outstanding contributor to the cultural scene in Central America, she is the author of numerous collections of poetry as well as of short stories and novels.

SILVINA OCAMPO (Argentina, 1903) is one of the members of *Sur* and one of the most distinguished Argentine women writers. Known for her themes dealing with the fantastic, she has been a long-time collaborator of Jorge Luis Borges and of her husband, Adolfo Bioy Casares. Her most recent work is *Cornelia Frente al Espejo* (1988).

ELVIRA ORPHÉE (Argentina, 1930) is the author of novels, short stories and journalistic prose. She is known in the United States for her novel *The Angel's Last Conquest*, which depicts the years of the "Dirty War" in Argentina. She was awarded a Guggenheim Fellowship for 1988-89.

NELIDA PIÑON (Brazil, 1937) is a novelist and journalist whose work has attained a vast readership in Brazil. Her novels include *Sala de Armas* (1973) and *Tebas do Meu Coreacao* (1974).

ELENA PONIATOWSKA (Mexico, 1923) is a journalist, and fiction writer who came to Mexico at the age of ten. She is the author of many books including *Hasta no verte, Jesus mio* and *Todo empezo en domingo*.

AMALIA RENDIC (Chile, 1928-1988) is considered to be one of the most outstanding authors of children's literature. She also wrote one novel, *Pasos Sonambulos* (1969).

LAURA RIESCO (Peru, 1940) is the author of the widely acclaimed novel *El Truco de los Ojos*. She is presently teaching at the University of Maine at Orono.

CRISTINA PERRI ROSSI (Uruguay, 1941) is a novelist, short story writer, poet, and journalist who was a political exile for many years in Barcelona, Spain. She is considered to be one of the most vocal voices of Uruguayan narrative and literature.

ALICIA STEIMBERG (Argentina, 1933) is the author of four novels as well as a collection of short stories. Along with Elvira Orphée, she is one of the most outstanding writers living in Argentina today.

LYGIA FAGUNDES TELLES (Brazil, 1923) is considered to be one of Brazil's greatest living writers, and the most widely translated. *The Three Marias* is one of her most well-known works.

LUISA VALENZUELA (Argentina, 1938) is one of the most prolific writers of her generation, as well as one of the most translated. Her most recent novel is *The Lizard's Tale*, translated from the Spanish by Gregory Rabassa.

The Translators

SUSAN BASSNETT is a poet as well as a literary critic. She is a senior lecturer at the University of Warwick, as well as an author of many critical works. Her most recent publication is *Feminist Experiences.*

MIRIAM BEN-UR, a Wellesley College graduate, majored in Spanish and Latin American Studies. She has lived in both the United States and Israel and now works as a free-lance translator in Boston.

LINDA BRITT teaches Latin American literature at Bates College and is working on a translation of the work of Carmen Naranjo.

CELESTE KOSTOPULOS-COOPERMAN teaches Spanish at Brandeis University and has just published a critical study of Maria Luisa Bombal.

JANET GOLD resides in Maine and is completing her doctorate in Spanish at the University of Massachusetts at Amherst.

ELAINE DOROUGH JOHNSON is a professor of Spanish at Augustana College. She is beginning to translate the work of Marta Brunet.

DAWN JORDAN is a translator of Brazilian literature and is currently translating the work of several Brazilian writers.

CHRISTOPHER LELAND, a professor of English at Bennington College, is also a novelist and author of *Mrs. Randall, the Boots of Marvels.* He has written a work on Argentine literature of the 1920s titled *The Last Happy Man.*

ALEXIS LEVITAN's translations of Clarice Lispector's stories won the 1984 Van de Bovenkamp-Armand G. Erpf International Award, given by the Translation Center, Colombia University.

SHARON MAGNARELLI, a professor of Spanish at Albert Magnus College, has written extensively on Valenzuela's work, as well as the work of other Latin American women writers, in her collection *The Spare Rib.*

JANICE MOLLOY is an editor at D.C. Heath. She has translated numerous articles by Marjorie Agosin and a collection of her essays.

GIOVANNI PONTIERO is a professor of Latin American literature at the University of Manchester, England, and one of the most outstanding translators of Brazilian fiction. He has translated many of the works of Clarice Lispector.

JOY RENJILIAN-BURGY is a tenured lecturer in the Spanish Department at Wellesley College. She is the co-editor of the anthology, *Album.*

LORRAINE ELENA ROSES is a professor of Spanish at Wellesley College and a specialist in Cuban literature. She is the author of *Voices of A Storyteller: Cuba's Lino Novas Calvo.*

NINA M. SCOTT, is a professor of Spanish at the University of Massachusetts. A specialist in Sor Juana Ines de la Cruz, she has just edited *Breaking Boundaries*, a collection of essays dealing with contemporary Hispanic women writers.

NANCY SAPORTA STERNBACH is a professor of Spanish at Smith College. Together with Nina Scott, she collaborated on the book *Breaking Boundaries*.

CLAUDIA VAN DER HEUVEL is a graduate student at the University of Massachusetts, Amherst. She is working on Nelida Pinon's fiction.

ALISON WEBER is a professor at the University of Virginia and the author of works on Latin American writers.